The Feast of Catchville

Scott F. Falkner

StoneGarden.Net Publishing
http://www.stonegarden.net

The Feast of Catchville. Copyright © 2006 Scott F. Falkner

ISBN: 1-60076-011-2

StoneGarden.Net Publishing

3851 Cottonwood Dr.

Danville, CA   94506

First StoneGarden.Net Publishing paperback printing: March 2006

First StoneGarden.net Publishing ebook printing: March 2006

Visit StoneGarden.Net Publishing on the web at http://www.stonegarden.net.

To find out more about Scott F. Falkner, "step into the strange" at www.scottfalkner.com.

This book is dedicated to my wife, Lisa…

…because she puts up with it.

March 31st, 2007

New York City, New York

12:04 p.m. EST

The boiling water in the teakettle started to scream, startling the woman from her doze. She scrambled off the dilapidated sofa and walked into the apartment's kitchen. Later, lying on her back on the linoleum floor with a gun barrel pressed to her head, she would think about how coincidental it was that the kettle started to steam at this very moment.

She took the pot off the burner and happened to look out the window to the street below at the same time. At high noon, the stretch of sidewalk that ran in front of the stout brownstone was usually crowded with pedestrian traffic. It was mostly the office workers from 35th working their way south to the food court on 26th. What caught the woman's attention weren't the people that were moving, but the man who wasn't.

There was nothing in particular about the man that marked him as different. In dress, he appeared *in place*. His black suit and briefcase matched those of the people that were pushing by him in hurried paces. But there *was* something different about this man, the woman was sure of it. For starters, he was standing still on the walk, looking alternately from a piece of white paper in his hand to the front door of the brownstone, like a salesman double checking an address.

As the woman's hand went to turn off the burner, the man looked up to her second story window. The two of them locked eyes for only a moment, but the woman saw all she needed. With a short gasp, she stepped away from the stove and out of the man's eyeshot.

The woman knew that it was most likely futile, but she still went over and put the chain on the door. A surge of questions ran through her mind as she moved into the living room. *How?* That was the big one. How did this man—whoever he was—find her? She'd been meticulous about covering her tracks. She'd changed her name. She'd changed her appearance. She'd resisted every urge she had to contact her friends and family. There'd be plenty of time after the act of revenge was accomplished to get back in touch with everyone. With all her precautions, she didn't really exist…

…and yet, somehow, someone had found her.

The next question that fired off in her mind was what to do about it. The apartment held little that she could use for a weapon, and there was nothing more *complicated* that she could prepare in so little time. Escape was something else that she only entertained briefly. The woman had a sense that even if she went to the back door and made her way down the fire escape, when she got to the bottom, the man would be there, waiting for her. To follow her this far, halfway across the United States, the man knew what he was doing.

More importantly, the man knew who she was; the man knew *what* she was.

Maybe she could use that to her benefit? Maybe she could explain to this man exactly why she'd done what she'd done? She had plenty of horror stories to draw from. Perhaps she could tell him a few of the darker ones. Perhaps he might understand.

Folding her arms in front of her chest, she listened. She strained her ears and realized she could hear the dim thump of footsteps on the stairs. The lock on the door that led to the street hadn't stopped him. No. The woman had a feeling that *no* lock would stop this one. She glanced at the phone, wondering if a call to the police would do any good. She was genuinely frightened for the first time in a long time. This wasn't how it was supposed to go! She hadn't done anything wrong! *She* was the victim!

More thoughts about self-preservation came to her now— should she grab an iron skillet or a steak knife from the rack in the kitchen? Should she...

WHAM!

The woman clutched a hand to her chest as the sound of a shoulder being thrown into the apartment door reached her ears.

WHAM!

This time the woman heard the wood of the door begin to splinter. Gods! The strength he must have!

WHAM!

Backing up on instinct, the back of the woman's legs struck the couch and she sat.

WHAM!

This time the door lock gave. But the door didn't open. The chain still held... but for how long?

From the <u>Cavalier Courier</u>

Cavalier, North Dakota

October 12th, 2006

AQUARIUM BURGLARIZED

-Ken Leavy

Police were called to the FINS & THINGS fish store at 221 Crescent Street this morning by storeowner Owen Clarke. Upon arriving to the store Clarke discovered that one of the windows in the back of the building was smashed. Police Officer Gary Menden told the Courier that when he arrived, "We found something mighty strange." The store's cash register and safe remained untouched. No graffiti or other acts of vandalism were discovered. It wasn't until Clarke performed an impromptu inventory that he discovered what had been taken. "I just don't understand it," Clarke commented, "why would someone take a puffer fish?" The storeowner was referring to a one-pound Fugu Puffer fish native to Japan. "The fish retails for fifteen ninety-nine. I don't see why someone would break a hundred dollar window to steal a sixteen dollar fish." When asked about that, Officer Menden replied, "It takes all kinds." As of this printing there are no leads in the mysterious theft. Anyone with any information is encouraged to call Crimestoppers.

From the <u>Cavalier Courier</u>

Cavalier, North Dakota

October 21st, 2006

RURAL ACCIDENT LEAVES ONE DEAD

-Michelle Tandy

Heavy rain is presumed to have caused yesterday's deadly accident on northbound Highway 18, just south of Cavalier. The driver, twenty-eight-year-old Margarite Kail, lost control of her car just past mile marker 115, went into the ditch and struck a telephone pole. The driver's husband, twenty-nine-year-old Timothy Kail, was thrown from the car and killed on impact. Margarite Kail was delivered via ambulance to Pembina County Hospital and released with only minor injuries. Investigators revealed that the driver was wearing her seatbelt, but the passenger was not. At present, alcohol is not believed to have been a factor.

From the Cavalier Courier

Cavalier, North Dakota

October 22nd, 2006

PEMBINA MORGUE LOSES BODY

-Ken Leavy

Pembina County Hospital officials in Cavalier contacted police this morning after it was discovered that a body was missing from the County Morgue. Timothy Kail (29) was killed earlier this week in an automobile accident on Highway 18. Kail's body was being held at the morgue pending an autopsy scheduled for this morning. Police refused to comment on the missing body, but the *Courier* has discovered that after closing down the Pembina County facility and conducting a search of its own, the body remains unfound. A total of four employees at the morgue have been on duty since Kail was deposited there earlier this week. All four employees have been detained by the Cavalier Police Department for questioning.

Margarite Kail, the deceased's widow, was unavailable for comment.

February 13th, 2007

County Trunk Highway 73, Wisconsin

2:51 p.m. CST

"Be careful, Seth."

As Seth Landon imagined his knuckles going white underneath his winter gloves, he mused that his wife really didn't have to encourage any extra care. The Volvo's windshield wipers slapped back and forth, but they did little to improve the view. Leaning forward, Seth looked up through the window. The sky was featureless, just a dark gray expanse beyond the ragged snarl of naked tree limbs that covered the road in an arthritic canopy. Seth leaned back and glanced at the speedometer. The red needle hovered between twenty-five and thirty. The last sign he remembered seeing said that the speed limit was fifty-five, but going the speed limit in this freezing rain would be suicide.

Seth slowed as they approached a wide, rambling corner. Even at a crawl the wheels of the station wagon threatened to slip. The problem was that they couldn't see the ice on the pavement. There were no slippery stretches. The road in front of them was completely covered with ice… or so Seth thought.

The drive up from Eau Claire had been uneventful, even pleasant. Though the northwestern part of Wisconsin had been plagued with a torrent of snow over the first part of the winter, the temperature took an upswing after New Year's, and melted much of it. Highway 53 had been clear and dry. It wasn't until they'd turned off of it near Gordon and headed east that the weather had started to turn. The rain started out as a light mist, but quickly turned into a downpour. For the last sixty or so miles, they'd seen nothing but woods and rain.

"How much farther?" Anne asked through gritted teeth.

"Not very… I don't think." In truth, Seth only had a vague idea how much farther they had to go. He glanced down again at the speedometer and worried about their speed. These days the sun set just before five. He really wanted to get to Catchville before the temperature dropped to well below freezing and everything really froze over. Seth guessed that they were only about forty miles from the small town, but at twenty-five miles an hour… well, the math just wasn't working out in their favor.

We should have left earlier, Seth thought, though the thought was moot. He certainly couldn't blame Anne for the late start. Sure, she'd been grading papers all morning, but he'd had his own work to finish up before they'd left Eau Claire. All of the English Department professor's at the university were required to turn in a syllabus for every course they'd be teaching in the following year by February sixteenth. Anne had completed hers over the Christmas break, but Seth had put it off, thinking that over the holidays he wanted to be as far away from work as possible. This morning, however, as he'd plowed through the syllabuses for five different courses, he wished that he'd followed his wife's lead.

"What's that?" Anne asked, pointing towards the side of the road. Seth read the sign as it approached: CATCHVILLE 22 MILES.

"Wow," Anne commented. "I didn't think that we were that close." She had a Wisconsin road map unfurled on her lap. "And at…" she leaned over and looked at the speedometer, "…twenty-six miles an hour, that puts us about an hour out."

Seth grinned. "I sure hope it's worth all this."

Anne heard the doubt in his voice. "Now, now, don't get all pessimistic just yet." She reached down and picked up a thin brochure from the purse between her feet. On the brochure's cover was a black and white picture of a rustic hotel. To Seth, the Bennington looked like the kind of hotel you'd see in a Clint Eastwood Western. Two stories tall, the place was a simple rectangular structure with a wide porch that wrapped around the front.

"Twenty-two beautiful rooms in a wilderness setting provide a relaxing getaway in scenic Catchville, Wisconsin," Anne read. "Enjoy long walks in the woods, take a swim in Farthing Pond in the summer or ice skate in the winter, relax with a book next to the fireplace or enjoy a home-cooked meal in our spacious dining room."

Seth couldn't contain a wide grin, "Sounds absolutely quaint."

Anne ignored his comment as she continued to read. "Open year round. Reservations are taken but not necessary…"

"That's something I'm thinking we should've done," Seth said. "What if we get up there and there's no vacancy?"

"In this weather?" Anne laughed. "I doubt it. Besides, you're the one who said it would be better if we didn't have a reservation. I believe your rationale was, and I quote, '*that we could leave if the place turned out to be a dump*'."

Seth slowed the Volvo as they approached another corner. "I don't think we'll be leaving tonight, no matter what the place looks like." As he spoke, Seth saw something on the right side of the road. His mind barely had time to register that the object blocking their way was a dead deer.

Pulling his foot off of the accelerator and easing the wheel to the left at the same time, Seth knew at once that they were going too fast for such a maneuver.

"Hang on!" he said as instinct kicked in. The rear end of the station wagon swung to the right as the car began to pivot counterclockwise. Everything seemed to go into slow motion as Seth relented to the uneasy fact that he no longer had control of the car. When the rear right tire hit the carcass the Volvo had slipped completely sideways on the road. The impact, though slight, now forced the station wagon to spin in the opposite direction. Seth's foot went to the brake pedal, but it was no use. The ice was glare and the car slid around until the rear end went off of the shoulder and into the ditch.

"Are you all right?" Seth asked when they jolted to a stop. Anne nodded but said nothing. A heavy gloom fell over them as the wipers slashed back and forth over the windshield.

"Are you sure you're okay?" Seth asked again.

"I'm all right. Are we stuck?"

Looking out the window, Seth saw that the car was half on and half off the road. They were sitting at an angle as the rear end of the car was down in the ditch. Seth held his breath and gently pushed down on the accelerator. They both heard the grinding hum of the front wheels spinning on the shoulder.

Seth put the Volvo into park and opened his door. He squinted at once through the pelting rain and almost fell as soon as he stepped out of the car. Sighing, he realized he'd been absolutely right about the road being covered with ice. A thin coat of it covered everything, even the dirt on the shoulder. He carefully stepped up to the front of the car and then to the rear. On inspection, the station wagon seemed fine. There wasn't even a mark where the tire had hit the deer. The problem was going to be getting the front tires to find any sort of traction on the ice.

Shaking his head to rid it of the rain, Seth got back into the car. Anne was holding their cell phone in her hand and shaking her head. "I can't get a signal." She held the phone up near the window and watched its display for a few more seconds. "Nope."

A slew of thoughts fell over Seth's mind all at once. The gas gauge indicated that they had about a quarter of a tank left; how long would it take to idle through the last of it? The last town they'd passed had been more than an hour back, and walking on this ice was going to be difficult. The cell phone didn't work. He couldn't remember the last time they'd seen a car on the road… so the odds of someone coming along to assist them were slim.

The facts made themselves perfectly clear. Seth and Anne were on their own.

February 13th, 2007

County Trunk Highway 73, Wisconsin

3:37 p.m. CST

Seth and Anne sat in the car as the terror of the situation took hold. Seth had tried shoving the blanket from their backseat underneath the front tires of the car, but it was no use. The angle at which the Volvo sat was too extreme. The amount of purchase the front tires would have to find in order to pull the car from its predicament could not be accomplished with something so insignificant as a blanket. He'd then pushed on the car, rocking it, while Anne gunned the gas pedal. When that didn't work, Seth walked up the road about a half a mile in both directions with the cell phone, trying to see if he couldn't get a signal. On his westerly jaunt, Seth got a closer look at the deer carcass in the road. He found it strange that the only indication of damage to the animal's body was its head. It looked like the deer's brain had exploded within its skull. Seth bit his lip and moved away from the animal while unsuccessfully trying to rid his own brain of the image.

Desperation began to set in as Seth tried using the tire jack to chip away at the ice around the tires. Ten minutes later, his gloves soaked and his hands cold, he admitted the futility of the action and got back in the car.

"Maybe you should shut off the engine? If we're going to be out here all night, we should conserve gas." Anne sounded like someone who'd reluctantly come to grips with a no-win situation.

Sighing, Seth weighed the pros and cons of shutting off the car in his mind. It was going to get very cold very quick if they didn't use the heater.

"The rain stopped," Anne said, causing Seth to look up. Indeed it had, although, as the two of them watched, the rain slowly gave over to snow. At first the flakes were tiny, raindrop-sized specks but in a matter of minutes they ballooned to the size of quarters. Seth and Anne watched in silence as the flakes started to accumulate on the hood of the Volvo.

"This isn't good," Seth whispered, as much to himself as to his wife.

Anne forced a small smile. "Someone will come along… won't they?"

Seth looked at the digital clock built into the dashboard. He gauged that they had maybe an hour before it was full on dark.

"Won't they, Seth?" Anne repeated.

He forced a pained smile and he reached out to touch her hands. "Yeah, someone will come."

February 13th, 2007

County Trunk Highway 73, Wisconsin

4:26 p.m. CST

The gas gauge now sat at a little over an eighth of a tank. As they sat in the car, the wind picked up, turning the area around the stranded Volvo into a veritable whiteout. The car rocked slightly at the more persistent gusts, and the ever present howl of the wind was starting to bite at both Seth and Anne's nerves. Seth tried tuning in something—anything—on the radio to try and drown out the sound of the wind, but found only static on both the am and fm dials.

Seth started to think about things that would've seemed crazy less than a half-hour ago. How much food and water did they have on hand? How cold was it really going to get in the car if the two of them had to spend the night out here? Would they survive? *Could* they survive?

Between the gusts of wind, they both saw that the snowflakes had increased in size. Falling out of the sky at a dizzying pace, they looked like hunks of ash being thrown from some distant fire or volcano. The road was now covered with a thin blanket of white. To their right, the deer that had put them into this mess was turning into a white hump at the edge of the road.

"Seth! Look!" Anne pointed to the right. At first Seth thought that she was just pointing out the snow cover on the deer carcass. It took him a moment to register the headlights coming around the wide corner.

"Thank God!" Seth cried, opening his door. He stood up outside of the car and waved a gloved hand over his head, hearing the grating groan of a diesel engine as he did. The dump truck that that engine belonged to slowed around the corner until it was moving at no more than a crawl. A large snowplow was anchored to the front of the truck, and as it approached, the driver of the truck used the plow to push the deer carcass into the far ditch.

Seth was still waving his hand as the truck came to a stop across the road. He could now see that the truck's tires were fitted with heavy chains. When the driver climbed out of the cab, the snow was coming down in such a flurry that Seth didn't get a good look at him until he was halfway to the Volvo.

"Hey there!" the big man yelled over the din. He wore a green parka over a pair of snow pants. His Sorel boots left wide tracks in the snow as he came.

Seth smiled at the man. "Boy, am I glad to see you."

The man nodded as he took in the stranded car. "Didn't listen to the weather report, did ya?"

"Pardon?" Seth wasn't sure he'd heard the man correctly.

"There's a lake effect warning," the man yelled, gesturing to the sky. "This shit's only gonna get worse. Where ya headed?"

"Catchville."

The man rubbed his snow-covered beard with a black mitten. "How much gas ya got left?"

"About an eighth of a tank, I think."

"All right," the man nodded. "I'll get a chain and pull you out. I'm headed up to Sanborn, north of Catchville. You can follow me up."

Seth nodded and was about to thank the man, but the driver was already walking back towards the truck.

February 13th, 2007

County Trunk Highway 73, Wisconsin

4:41 p.m. CST

Seth clenched his teeth when the Volvo's front axle groaned under the pull of the chain connected to the dump truck, but after driving for a few miles, the car seemed fine.

Anne and Seth were certainly breathing easier as they moved slowly down the rural highway, but there was still an air of anxiety between them. The snow and wind hadn't dissipated in the least; in fact it had intensified. It was clear that they were smack dab in the middle of a full-blown blizzard. Anne teased Seth as they drove, trying to dispel that awkward, ominous sensation that they both felt. "How quaint does the Bennington look now?" she jabbed. Seth gave her a short laugh, but he never once took his eyes off the road. The driver of the truck had been nice, a Godsend really, but Seth didn't want to push his luck by going into the ditch again. He was determined to keep a slow and steady pace behind the plow until they reached Catchville.

February 13th, 2007

Catchville, Wisconsin

5:01 p.m. CST

Anne was the first to spot the Amoco sign. Between the whirling snow and the absolute dark, the light wasn't visible until they were almost beneath it. Seth didn't put his foot on the brake but did take it off the accelerator as he followed the dump truck into the gas station. The driver gave a short blast on the truck's air horn before continuing back onto the road.

Seth pulled in front of the station's lone gas pump and sighed. "Well, we made it."

"Yeah," Anne said uneasily. She looked through the windshield trying to see anything else in the town, but the blizzard had cut down visibility to less than a few dozen yards.

"Let's go inside." Seth was assaulted by the wind as soon as he opened the car door. Unhooking the gas pump, he inserted it into the Volvo's tank and followed Anne into the station.

"You two is lucky Mack was out there," the middle-aged man behind the counter said when they walked through the door. The glare of the overhead fluorescents made Seth and Anne squint as they took in the station. A single rack ran down the center of the store and held everything from beef jerky to toilet paper to motor oil. Along the left side of the store were several refrigerators with sliding glass doors containing soda and beer. The rear of the station held two doors for the bathrooms, and the far wall held a counter hooded with cigarette racks.

Seth and Anne stomped the snow from their feet on the mat inside the door. Anne then retreated to the rear of the store to use the restroom. "How's that?" Seth asked, approaching the counter.

A barstool sat on the customer side of the counter, and on it sat a codger of about seventy. A cigarette smoldered between his lips and a lopsided John Deere hat sat on his head. The man behind the counter wore a flannel shirt. Tufts of gray hair sprouted out above his ears on his otherwise bald head.

"I say you two was lucky you ran into Mack," The man with the tufts gestured out the window with his hand. "This ain't the night to be running solitaire without so much as a pair of snow chains."

The old man on the barstool removed the cigarette from his mouth long enough to suffer through an agonizing coughing spat, and then placed it back on his lip.

Seth took off his winter hat and nodded. "We went in the ditch a ways southwest of here. That guy pulled us out, otherwise I think we would've been stuck there all night."

"Sure as shit," the geezer on the barstool said in a gravelly voice. "Lake effect. It'll be a bastard. Worst in years."

"Yeah?" Seth answered, smiling inward at the local flavor of the place.

"Don't let 'em scare ya," the clerk commented. "Dizzy says they're all gonna be the worst in years."

Seth watched the cigarette smoke whirl around the codger's head as he spoke. "This one's a creakin', though. I can feel it, young fella. Lake effect always rattles the 'thritis." He held out his arm as if to demonstrate something that Seth didn't quite catch.

The clerk smiled. "At any rate, looks like you folks will be stuck in Catchville for a while."

"That's okay. We were headed here anyway."

Both of the locals attempted to hide their shock at Seth's comment, but neither did a very good job. "You got relations here?" the man with the cigarette asked.

Seth shook his head as Anne walked back up from the

restroom. "We were planning on staying at the Bennington Hotel."

Again, shock registered in the two men's eyes. The smoker grunted and the clerk turned his attention to the gas pump monitor. "Gas is done."

Seth pulled out his wallet as Anne spoke up. "Where exactly is the Bennington?"

The codger slung his thumb over his shoulder. "Just about a hundred yards down the road on this side of the street. It's a big old monstrosity, sticks out like a garish tombstone. You can't miss it... though, maybe in this weather you could. Heh!"

Anne smiled despite the description. "Doesn't sound like you think too much of the hotel?"

The old man shrugged, took a weak drag from his smoke and put it out in an aluminum ashtray on the counter.

"Twenty-four oh eight," the clerk read the gas monitor out loud.

"You want anything?" Seth asked Anne as he paid cash for the gas.

She smiled. "A hot shower."

The clerk gave Seth back his change and pointed out the window. "You'll want to head over to the tavern just up that way. It's across the street from the Bennington. You'll find Maggie inside."

Seth and Anne exchanged a confused look. "Uh, Maggie?" Seth asked.

"She owns the hotel," the clerk said. "And the tavern too. She'll be tending bar."

"So... there's no one at the hotel?" Anne asked.

The codger let loose a quick, loud laugh that made them jump. "We don't get much for visitors here in Catchville, Miss. If Mags didn't have the tavern, she wouldn't have much of nothin'."

Anne seemed ready to press the subject but Seth decided he'd had enough of the two men. He pocketed his change and gently pulled on his wife's arm. "All right, then. Thanks. Have a good night."

February 13th, 2007

Catchville, Wisconsin

5:13 p.m. CST

Seth moved the car to the edge of the Amoco parking lot and looked both ways. The wind and snow were so severe now that he couldn't really see more than ten feet in either direction.

"I hope nothing's coming." Seth pulled out onto the road. Both of them sat in silence as the Volvo crept down what amounted to the main street of Catchville. The sparse streetlights didn't do much to improve their vision, but they did allow them to catch glimpses of two houses on the same side of the street as the gas station. Both homes were simple, single-story dwellings, and both looked like they'd seen better days. So far, it didn't appear that there were any sidewalks in the town. The short driveways of each house reached right out to the highway. They passed some sort of closed business on the right side of the street. The sign out front was masked with snow, so they couldn't read it, but like the houses, the store looked ill kept.

"It's like a ghost town," Anne said, shaking her head.

Both of them saw the tavern at the same time. It was on the right side of the highway and the spotlights at the corners of its parking lot were barely visible from the road. Another light shone atop a pole near the shoulder. The sign held the emblem for Grain Belt beer at its top, and beneath that in bold, black letters, it read: MAGGIE'S TAVERN. The wind blew the sign back and forth wildly.

Seth pulled the Volvo into the snow-covered lot.

"Here's the bar," he said, "but where's the…." Both he and Anne looked back across the highway. A dim light in a window showed them the approximate location of the Bennington Hotel, but the snow was just too thick to make out any details.

"It looks like they've got vacancies," Seth said with a smile.

He parked next to an old pickup that was one of three cars in the lot. Parked very near to the tavern's door were two snowmobiles, each of which had close to six inches of snow accumulated on their seats.

Other than the small, diamond shaped one in the front door, the tavern held no windows, so Seth and Anne didn't know what to expect as they walked inside. The soft sounds of some contemporary country-western singer came from the jukebox on the far side of the immense room. Maggie's Tavern was much more spacious than its exterior had led them to believe. A pool table was the centerpiece of the open space. Six wooden booths ran along the left wall. Judging from the menus tucked between the ketchup bottles and napkin dispensers, Maggie's served as Catchville's diner as well as its watering hole. A slew of barstools lined the ancient bar on right side of the room. Behind the bar were three racks jammed with a bottle of what seemed like every hard liquor known to man. Between the racks were mirrors that reflected the whole of the bar and made the space seem larger than it really was.

The four patrons sitting at the bar turned to look at Seth and Anne as they entered. The two closest to them—a man and a woman, both in their forties—were presumably the owners of the snowmobiles. Each of them wore an expensive snowmobile suit stripped back to their waists. Their hats and mittens sat on the bar in front of them next to their beers. Two other drinkers sat down at the other end of the bar. One of the men appeared to be in his mid-twenties and the other looked twice that; both men looked right at home.

A woman with graying hair pulled back into a tight bun stood behind the bar wearing a white apron over her turtleneck. She looked up from the beer glasses she was washing long enough to say, "Come on in. I'll be right with ya'," before drying her hands with a rag and moving back through a set of metal swinging doors. Anne and Seth picked out a pair of stools midway down the bar, took off their jackets, and sat.

"Would you kill me if I said I'd like to get something to eat before we go over to the hotel?" Seth asked.

Anne smiled. "Hey, vacation or no vacation, a man's gotta eat."

The bartender came back through the swinging doors. As she passed the two men to Seth and Anne's left, the woman gestured to the near-empty pitcher between them. "You two need another?"

"Does it look like we're going anywhere, Mags?" the older of the two men answered. He turned and smiled at Anne as he spoke. She forced a weak smile of her own and turned away.

"And what can I get you two?" the bartender asked.

Seth was the one who answered. "Are you Maggie?"

"I am," the woman said with suspicion on her lips. "Who's askin'?"

Smiling, Seth gestured to himself and Anne. "We were just in the gas station up the block and the clerk said we should ask for you."

While Seth spoke, Maggie placed both of her hands on the bar and moved her eyes back and forth between the two of them.

Anne explained. "We want to stay at the hotel… at the Bennington."

"Oh," she said, smiling. "Where are you two headed?"

Anne and Seth looked at each other, confused. "Uh…" Seth started, "…like my wife said, we'd like to stay at the hotel. At the Bennington."

Maggie tapped her fingers on the bar. Her smile was gone. "Let me see if I got this straight. You two came to Catchville to specifically stay at the hotel across the street?"

"That's right," Seth said. Anne reached down and rummaged through the pockets of her jacket. While she did, Maggie and the two men at the end of the bar exchanged confused looks.

"Here," Anne said, finding what she was looking for. She pulled out the Bennington brochure and sat in on the bar. Maggie's eyes widened when she saw it. Carefully, as if she were handling some sort of medieval artifact, the bartender picked up the brochure.

Maggie shook her head as she looked at it. "Well, I'll be damned. Skip, you've got to take a look at this."

"What is it, Mags?" Maggie stepped down and placed the brochure on the bar. The two locals leaned in to take a look.

"That's a bit-o-history right there, that is," the older man said—Maggie had called him Skip. "Was that when you took over, Mags, or is that somethin' your dad put out?"

Maggie turned over the brochure and continued to examine it. "I sure didn't have anything to do with it." She looked up at Anne. "Where'd you get this, Miss?"

Anne blushed faintly as all eyes in the bar turned on her. "I found it after class. We're professors at the university in Eau Claire. I assumed one of my students dropped it. We thought it looked like a nice place to spend the weekend."

Seth jumped in. "The hotel's still open, I hope."

Maggie smiled. "Oh, it's open all right. But if you two are looking for the Bennington that's here in the brochure, I'm afraid you're going to be sorely disappointed."

Anne and Seth's spirits sank as Maggie continued. "My dad opened the hotel in 1919. I took over when he died in 'seventy. When I got her, the Bennington had been downhill for going on a decade."

"When's that from, then?" Seth asked, pointing at the

brochure.

Maggie shook her head as she looked at it. "There's no date, but I'm guessing it's got to be from the sixties."

"At least!" Skip chimed in.

"My dad made one last push around sixty-five to try and drum up business. This might be one of the fruits of his labors." She handed the brochure back to Anne.

Anne sighed, "You do have vacancies, though. Don't you?"

Maggie tipped her head back and laughed. After a moment the two men at the end of the bar joined in with her. "My yes," Maggie finally said, wiping the corners of her eyes with her thumb. "We've got vacancies, all right. The Bennington's *always* got vacancies." She gestured down the bar to the two snowmobilers. "And you won't be alone. Those two will be staying too."

Seth and Anne looked down the bar. The man and woman so far hadn't said anything—not even to each other—but to Seth it seemed like the two of them were just itching to join in on the conversation. The woman had tight, black curly hair that threatened to grow into a beehive. Seth could smell the woman's perfume from where he sat; it was thick, tangy stuff that smelled like it was bought at J.C. Penny's or Walgreen's. Between the woman's dangly earrings, long gold necklace and sparkling red sweater, she looked like she was more suited to attending a holiday party than hitting the trails. Her husband held up his near-empty beer mug to acknowledge Anne and Seth. A big burly man, his curly hair matched his blonde goatee.

"How-do!" the man said, somehow sounding a bit too jovial. "We was running our sleds from Cable up to Ashland. I knew it was a long push, but I think we would've made it if the weather hadn't turned. I'm Jim Pruitt by the way. This is my wife, Nancy."

The woman gave them a wide smile. "We're from

Hayward!" she said enthusiastically.

"We're the Landon's. Seth and Anne," Seth said. "Pleased to meet you."

The song on the jukebox ended, and before the next one started they all listened to the wind howling outside against the eaves. It was an eerie sound that made Anne think of just how far out in the woods they actually were.

"I suppose you two will be staying as well?" Maggie looked down at the two men to Anne's left.

"Yup," the one named Skip said. "By the sounds of things I'd say you're right. Driving back up to Sanborn in this mess seems out of the question."

The bartender shook her head. "How you two manage to get stranded in my bar every time there's a storm I'll never know. It's almost like you plan it."

The man sitting next to Skip gave a grunt. "Who says we don't plan it? How 'bout another pitcher, Maggie?"

She stepped down and picked up their empty. "If it'll shut you up, Ronnie, sure thing."

Seth grabbed a menu that was lying on the counter while Anne once more perused the Bennington's brochure. "What'll it be?" Seth asked.

"Huh?"

He looked over and saw the expression of disdain on her face as she looked at the black and white picture of the hotel. "Hey," he said, mustering as much compassion as he could, "it's still a vacation, right?"

The corner of Anne's mouth upturned in the slightest.

"So," Seth leaned over and whispered in her ear, "we'll have some supper, get a room, and then do what we came here to do."

The corner of her mouth upturned some more.

"And if the place really sucks," Seth continued, "we'll check out first thing in the morning and make a bee-line for the Holiday Inn in Eau Claire. Deal?"

Now he got a full-blown smile. "Deal," she said, and sat the brochure off to the side.

"So," Maggie returned to their area of the bar, "what can I get you two?"

"You decide," Seth said to Anne.

"Um, how about two cheeseburgers, a pitcher of Leinies and a large order of cheese curds."

The bartender nodded and turned her head towards the metal doors at the back of the bar. "Audrey," she called out, "two cheeseburgers and an order of curds." Before she was finished yelling out the order, a young girl of not more than nineteen came through the doors. Wearing a loose Green Bay Packers sweatshirt, the girl had enormous breasts and blonde bangs that were hair sprayed high up off of her forehead.

"I just finished wiping down the grill!" the girl hissed.

Maggie seemed to take no notice of her; she simply started pouring Seth and Anne's pitcher of beer.

When the girl realized the bartender wasn't going to answer her, she lightly stamped her foot on the floor, blew a burst of air through her lips, and stomped back into the kitchen.

"If it's any trouble..." Anne started, but the bartender shook her head.

"No trouble." She poured two glasses of beer and set them and the pitcher down on the bar. "My niece takes to work like a cat takes to water. Anyway, I don't know where she thinks she's going in this storm other than across the street. She's got a fella up in Sanborn, but there's no way she's gonna be gettin' up there tonight."

Seth nodded. "The guy down at the gas station said something about a lake effect storm?"

Skip was the one who answered. "Lake effects are the worst. You get a good wind outta the northwest this time of year, the storm picks up moisture outta Lake Superior and by the time it coasts back over dry land the clouds got enough in 'em to drop ten, twelve inches. Sometimes more."

"Often times more!" the man sitting next to Skip said. Seth thought he'd heard Maggie call him Ronnie.

"So, are they usually pretty good about plowing it out the next day?" Seth asked. Though Catchville seemed colorful enough, he was sure that he and Anne would be headed out in the morning if at all possible.

Skip shrugged. "It all depends on how long the storm lasts."

"Last year we had one... lasted four going on five days," Ronnie said, leaning forward so that he could see down the bar past his buddy.

The terror in Anne and Seth's faces must have been obvious because Maggie started shaking her head at once. "That's awfully rare, Ronnie. Usually the lake effects hit hard and then clear out. If it quits snowing by morning, Mack will have the highway cleared between Sanborn and Highway 63 by noon." Maggie leaned into the bar and pretended to whisper just to Seth and Anne. "Don't worry, you shouldn't be stuck with us any longer than you want to be."

Seth shook his head, embarrassed. "That's not what I meant..."

Maggie laughed. "Don't worry about it."

"Mack, he's the one that helped us out a bit ago," Seth said, and then, after some prompting from the others, he and Anne told the tale of how they'd gone off the road and been rescued by the snowplow. Seth laughed to himself as he realized that the situation sounded a lot less dire in hindsight than it did at the time.

"Don't take it lightly, young fella," Skip said at Seth's lightheartedness. "Plenty of folk die up here in the winter. It's just a fact of life. Lot's of snow as we often get, ridiculous temperatures that would make any animal with half a brain rethink its habitat..."

"What's that make you two, then?" Maggie chided.

Skip gave her a toothy grin. "That makes us no smarter than you, Mags." The bartender could only roll her eyes.

"That ice underneath it all sure don't help matters." The snowmobiler—Jim—said from the end of the bar. "Even if you've got a four-wheel drive, trying to get a grip on that snow-covered ice is next to impossible."

His wife, Nancy, nodded as she lit a cigarette. "That ice makes it hard even with the sleds. You've got to slow down so much before you make a turn. The skids just won't grab if they don't get deep in the snow, you know?"

Anne and Seth nodded though neither one of them had ever been on a snowmobile in their lives.

February 13th, 2007

Catchville, Wisconsin

5:56 p.m. CST

After they'd finished their burgers and beer, Maggie agreed to lead Seth and Anne, and the snowmobilers, Jim and Nancy, over to the hotel so they could all get settled in their rooms. They were just about to head out the door when Maggie stopped and turned around.

"Ronnie?"

The man was in mid-drink. He stopped and slowly turned on his barstool with raised eyebrows.

"I wonder if you'd go down and check on Mrs. Meadows for me?"

Ronnie's face scrunched up in dismay at once.

"Oh, come on now," Maggie persisted. "I hate to think of her in that tiny house all alone in this weather. Just go make sure she's got some candles and a flashlight."

Sighing, Ronnie shook his head. "I don't know why the hell it should be me that has to go check on the old witch."

Maggie crossed her arms. "When was the last time you paid your tab, Ronnie?"

The color dropped out of the man's face before he cleared his throat. "Let me finish another couple here, and then I'll head over."

Seth couldn't believe how bad the weather had gotten in just the short amount of time they'd spent in the bar. A heavy three or four inches of snow had accumulated on top of the Volvo while they were inside. The wind would blow hard for a few moments and then die down to almost nothing. In the light of the parking lot lampposts they saw nothing but a whitewash of snow.

"I'll meet you there!" Maggie yelled over a gust of wind. She hugged her jacket to herself and began across the lot. Seth was about to ask her if she wanted a ride to the hotel but the woman had already reached the road and was starting across. Using his glove as a scraper, Seth cleared as much snow as he could from the windshield and then got inside.

"This is crazy," Anne said, looking out the window.

"I know." Seth turned on the ignition and tried the wipers. They had little effect except to streak water and ice across the windshield. "I guess I can see well enough to get us across the road."

The two of them looked up as the sound of whining engines roared to life next to the bar. After a moment, the headlights of Jim and Nancy's snowmobiles moved across the lot.

"You don't think we're going to be stuck here all weekend, do you Seth?" Anne's face displayed a mixture of disappointment and fear.

He shook his head in response, though on the inside he really had no idea how long they'd be stranded in Catchville. "You heard Maggie, usually these storms don't last that long. The road will be cleared tomorrow, and then we can get out of here."

February 13th, 2007

Catchville, Wisconsin

6:09 p.m. CST

The hotel's parking lot was on the west side of the building. Once parked, Seth and Anne grabbed their suitcases from the trunk in a flurry and hustled to the Bennington's front porch where the awning provided at least a minor reprieve from the snow. The porch itself could've been considered rickety at best. Every step the two of them took produced creaks loud enough to be heard over the drone of the blowing wind. Just as they were fumbling to try and open up the front door, it flung open with Jim at its side.

"Come on in!" the big man said with a smile on his lips.

It was apparent how grand the large lobby of the Bennington might've been in its better days, but the white-painted woodwork on the ceilings and walls was flaking, and the hardwood floor had faded and warped through years of neglect. A pair of French doors on the far side of the lobby led into the dining room. To the right was an archway that led into a long hall, and to the left was the reception desk next to a wide staircase lined with tattered carpeting.

"Close the door tight," Maggie said, removing her mittens and hat behind the desk. "That catch has a tendency to come undone if it's not slammed tight."

Anne closed the front door hard behind them and then gave it a good pull to make sure it wouldn't come back open.

"Now then," Maggie pulled out a large, flat registry and sat it on the desk, "since you're all here I'll give you both the speech at the same time." She opened up a drawer behind her, pulled out two heavy-duty flashlights and sat them on the counter. Maggie gestured to them. "These are for you. Often times when we have a bad lake effect like this after a freezing rain, the power lines get into trouble and we'll lose power. You'll all find kerosene lanterns in your rooms and matches in the bedside drawers. I can't stress enough how important this is; keep your flashlights close to you at night. Don't fumble or fool around with the kerosene lanterns unless you can see what you're doing."

"What about heat?" Nancy asked. "Do you have wood heat?"

Maggie shook her head. "No, but we have a generator. It's a bit antiquated, and it's not hooked up so that'll work on the lights, but it'll keep us warm on the lower level until the lines get fixed. That brings me to the next point, down that hall behind you is where you'll find your rooms." She gestured to Jim and Nancy. "You two will be 101. And you two will be in 102."

Seth nodded before gesturing to the dining room. "I don't suppose you've got a five-star chef hiding back there?"

The woman gave him the smallest of smiles. "I'm afraid not, Mr. Landon. Audrey and I are the only staff. The dining room hasn't been open in a decade, though you're all welcome to go out and take in the view. The windows look over Farthing Pond. My bar is open late, and when there are guests here I open up the grill early for breakfast. Nothing fancy—hash browns, bacon, eggs and toast is about all you'll find—but it's better than nothing."

Jim and Seth signed the register and Maggie gave them their respective keys. "Your keys will work on the front door so you can come and go as you please, just make sure you shut the door tight behind ya." She slung a thumb over her shoulder. "My apartment is back there. Audrey's staying with me at the moment, so if you need either one of us and we're not over at the tavern, just give the bell a ring." Maggie pointed to a large golden bell sitting on the corner of the counter. "Once you're settled, I invite you to come on across the street and whoop it up with us. There's sure not much more to do on a night like this."

February 13th, 2007

Catchville, Wisconsin

6:41 p.m. CST

"Hey," Seth said, coming out of the bathroom with a towel wrapped around his waist. "That's quite the tub, huh? Clawed feet and all."

"Yeah," Anne smiled. She was lying on the room's bed in her bathrobe. "Quite the tub. Quite the hotel as a matter of fact."

Seth looked around at the room and sighed. "Not exactly Caesar's Palace, is it?"

Anne slunk down further on the bed and laid her head back on the flat pillow. She brought her hands up to her face. "God! Please let the roads be open tomorrow!"

Walking over, Seth sat on the edge of the bed. "Well, we're here so we might as well make the best of it... right?"

"How, Seth? There's nothing to do."

He reached out and touched her knee. "Well, there is this huge bed..."

Anne smiled at him. That *was* why they were here. "Rest and relaxation," was what Dr. Prine had told them, "then just let nature take its course."

"I guess this would be quite a story to tell."

Seth scrunched his eyebrows. "What do you mean?"

Reaching out, Anne ran her fingers through her husband's hair. "I mean if we do end up getting pregnant here, it'll make a good story."

Sitting up straight, Seth shook his head. "Come on, now.

You heard Dr. Prine. We're not supposed to be focusing on getting pregnant. That's probably our biggest problem. We're supposed to relax and just… go with the flow."

Anne chuckled. "Right. And how, pray tell, do we go with the flow?"

"Like this!" Seth stood up and pulled the towel away from his waist as Anne started to laugh. She laughed harder when he dove on top of her.

February 13th, 2007

Catchville, Wisconsin

7:08 p.m. CST

Maggie locked up the doorway to her apartment at the hotel and took one last look down the first floor hall. She'd waited around a bit after the two couples got settled to see if they had any questions or problems. It was almost a certainty that one or both of them would promptly complain about the lack of HBO or a swimming pool, or even a phone for that matter, but so far none of them had. She supposed that the discussion over at the tavern about the hotel falling out of sorts had something to do with it. The patrons already knew that they didn't have much to look forward to at the Bennington. Still, Maggie thought, without the Bennington, they'd all be without paddles in the middle of a storm that really did look to be the worst one in years.

Hurrying across the street, Maggie saw that the footprints she'd left in the snow only thirty minutes ago, were now gone.

When she opened the door of the tavern she saw that Less Huggard had given up the ghost down at the Amoco station. Dizzy Vaughn sat next to him, sucking on a cigarette as usual.

"Hey, Maggie!" Less said, turning on his barstool.

"Hello, Less. Close down the station?"

He nodded. "At this point anybody with a car ain't goin' nowhere. Me and Dizz' even walked down here. No use in goin' through all the hassle to clean the car off to drive half a block, is there?"

Maggie gave him a short smile as she walked around behind the bar. Audrey was in the process of pouring another pitcher for Skip and Ronnie. As the girl bent over to get them clean glasses, Maggie saw Ronnie trying to get a glimpse down the girls' shirt. "Ronnie?"

The man looked up, startled. "Yeah?"

"How's Mrs. Meadows doing?"

The man clasped his hand to his forehead. "Shit. I plumb forgot."

Audrey looked to her aunt, the pitcher of beer in her hand. Maggie shook her head. "Nope. Ronnie's cut off until he does what I asked him to do."

"Come on, Maggie," Ronnie whined. "The old lady's fine. She always comes out of these things on top, don't she? She must be, what, close to a hundred-years-old, and there ain't been a snowstorm that she hasn't survived yet."

Maggie took off her coat. "She's a good decade and a half short of a century, for your information, and you don't get another drop 'til you go check on her."

"Shit," Ronnie muttered. He grabbed his hat and gloves off of the bar and stood up to go.

February 13th, 2007

Catchville, Wisconsin

7:11 p.m. CST

Anne and Seth—both naked and sweaty—lay on their backs in a tangled mess of bedcovers, staring at the ceiling. "Yup," Seth commented, catching his breath. "That'll do it."

"Oh my God," Anne said, laughing at the same time.

Seth propped himself up on one elbow and looked at his wife. "What? I don't think there was anything *funny* about my performance!"

At that, Anne started laughing harder but shook her head. "I was just thinking that we've been trying to get pregnant for so long..." She laughed out loud once more, "...and now, if it happens here." Anne continued to laugh as a slow grin slid across Seth's mouth.

"That's not funny."

Anne laughed harder.

"That's not funny at all."

There was a sharp knock at the door and both of them looked at each other, startled. "Who's that?" Seth whispered.

Anne continued to giggle. "I doubt that it's room service." The comment only brought the giggles on harder and she brought the sheet up over her face in order to muffle them.

"Who is it?" Seth called out.

The answer from the door made Anne's giggles verge on laughter beneath the covers. "It's Jim! Jim Pruitt!"

Seth let out a chuckle himself as he jumped out of bed.

"Just a second, Jim." He pulled on a pair of pants and a tee shirt and went to the door.

"What can I do for you?" Seth asked, opening the door just far enough to stick his head out. Jim looked at him for a moment before giving a sly smile. Seth realized that the man was looking at his hair, which was almost certainly well mussed from he and Anne's *activities*. Seth quickly ran a hand through his hair in an attempt to mat it down.

"What's going on, Jim?"

"I, uh, didn't mean to interrupt anything..."

Seth shook his head. "Not at all. I just got out of the shower, er, I mean the bath."

"Oh. Well, me and Nancy are heading back over to the tavern and we wondered if you two wanted to walk over with us?"

"Uh..." Seth stammered, his hand still on top of his head, "...why don't you two go over and we'll be right along in a bit."

Jim nodded while giving Seth a stupid, knowing smile. "All right then. We'll see you there."

Seth closed the door and as soon as he did Anne's giggles burst out into gales of laughter, making the sheet quiver over her body. "That was Jim Pruitt," Seth said, and began to laugh himself. "He wanted to know if we wanted to go over to the bar with him."

Anne pulled down the covers. "Was Nancy with him?"

Putting his hands on his hips and shaking his head in mock thought, Seth said, "You know, I didn't see her, but I did smell her perfume... so that means that she's probably somewhere on this side of the street."

At that, Anne laughed so hard she had to wipe tears out of the corners of her eyes.

February 13th, 2007

Catchville, Wisconsin

7:19 p.m. CST

Walking east along the edge of the road, Ronnie Eaves stumbled and went down on one knee. It wasn't just because he was drunk, though drunk he was, the ice underneath the new snow was slicker than snot. "Dammit," he cursed under his breath. Standing back upright, Ronnie peered down at his knee to see if his jeans had ripped. He had to blink several times to bring the area he was looking at into focus, but the denim covering his kneecap still seemed to be in tact.

"What a bitch!" Ronnie exclaimed out into the night. He could have been talking about Maggie or the storm or even Mrs. Meadows. To Ronnie, at that moment, they were all one in the same. They were all blocking him from getting more beer.

Forcing one foot in front of the other, he continued to walk. Though he was only fifty yards or so north of Maggie's Tavern, the lights of the parking lot were no longer visible behind him. It was difficult to see through the swirling snow and it forced him to squint and keep his head down as he walked. The dip to his right indicated where the edge of the road was. As long as he stayed on the road, he'd eventually come to the old witch's house.

Maggie had made him go check on Mrs. Meadows many times before and he hated it. The lady was always fine, sitting there in that crappy old kitchen of hers next to the radiator, wrapped in an afghan and sipping tea, and she'd have the gall to get pissed at him when he asked if she was doin' okay. Why the hell did he have to freeze his ever-lasting butt off just to see if the old broad was all right when she didn't even want him there?

Why? Because if he didn't do it, Maggie would cut him off.

Well, the sooner he got to Mrs. Meadows' place, the sooner he'd be parked on his barstool. Ronnie pulled his hat down over his ears a bit farther as a particularly strong gust of wind against his back forced him forward, as if it wanted him to hurry, too. He brought his eyes up to look ahead. The old lady's house couldn't be too much further on. Hell, the total area of Catchville was smaller than the size of a couple football fields, with Maggie's Tavern at its center. Any second now Ronnie expected to come to the thin driveway that led to Mrs. Meadows' garage.

About twenty yards ahead, through the star-field of snow, someone was standing at the edge of the road. Ronnie stopped. Who the hell was out in this mess? Had old lady Meadows finally gone off her rocker and started wandering around outside? He brought his gloved hand up to shield his eyes from the snow. No. Whoever it was, it was too tall to be Mrs. Meadows. Ronnie couldn't make out any features, but the figure ahead in the snow remained motionless, apparently watching him.

"Hey?" Ronnie said, his voice cracking. "Who's that?" He blinked and the figure moved off to the left and began running through the snow. "Hey!" Ronnie called after it, but the figure was gone into the night. Muttering to himself, Ronnie continued on towards Mrs. Meadows' place. He kept glancing to his left to look for any sign of the stranger, but saw none.

Walking up the driveway, Mrs. Meadows' kitchen light slowly became brighter. The old lady lived in a small house that was probably as old as she was. Three concrete steps led up to the unused front door. There was a door on the side of the house that faced the garage and that was where Ronnie headed. A few yards from the door he stopped. The snow had already drifted up to a foot deep along the front of the garage and swept over across the walk to the edge of the house. In that drift, indistinct because of the terrible wind, Ronnie saw several footprints leading across the front yard, towards the highway. Using his eyes, he followed the prints back to the side door of the house. The screen door was open and the wooden one beyond it was ajar.

Had it been old lady Meadows that Ronnie had seen out on the highway? No, his alcohol-addled mind reasoned. The figure he'd seen had moved much too quickly to be the elderly woman who had trouble getting up from her chair in the kitchen.

Feeling an overwhelming sense of dread, Ronnie forced one foot in front of the other and headed towards the door. Through the entrance, he could see the yellow glow from the light above the kitchen sink. The side door led straight into the kitchen, and that was where Ronnie expected to find Mrs. Meadows. But why had she left the door open?

"Shit," he cursed under his breath. Wouldn't that be just his luck, to find that the old witch had finally dropped dead of God-knew-what on tonight of all nights?

He gulped hard and stepped into the kitchen. "Mrs. Meadows?" he called out. If the witch wasn't dead she'd have a holy fit over Ronnie just walking into her home unannounced.

But there was no answer. The only sounds in the house were a deep hum caused by water circulating through the radiators and the wind beating against the walls. His hand still on the doorknob, Ronnie looked about the kitchen. The small house might have been packed from wall to wall with junk, but it *was* clean. Everything on the counter—from the coffee maker to the breadbox to the toaster oven to the coffee cup rack—was arranged in perfect, uniform order. The white cupboards above the counter all shone spotlessly, as if they'd been painted only yesterday. The same was true of the yellow and white checkered tile floor. For a lady who seemed to have a hard time just getting up out of her chair, she sure knew how to use a mop.

There was a closed door to the left that led down to the tiny cellar. The only other way out of the kitchen was through an archway on the far side that led into the living room. Ronnie craned his neck. "Mrs. Meadows?"

Sighing, Ronnie supposed he'd have to make his way through the house and see if she was even here. If she wasn't, if

Mrs. Meadows had left town with relatives or some such, Maggie was going to get an earful. But that didn't make any sense. If the lady was gone then why was her door open?

Ronnie moved carefully around the kitchen table to go into the living room when he stopped. The table had blocked his view of the vein-stricken white feet from where he'd stood by the door, but now they were in plain view. The body they belonged to, however, was in the darkened living room.

"Shit," Ronnie spat, realizing that his worst fears were coming to fruition before his very eyes. He went to move further around the table but his feet refused; instead, he leaned as far as he could to the right to see the rest of the woman's body. In the dim glow of the kitchen light, Ronnie could make out the hem of Mrs. Meadows' pink bathrobe below her thighs, but he couldn't see anything else. The rest of her was masked in the darkness of the living room. He let loose a low moan that came out as a terrified hum.

"Mrs. Meadows?" he tried once more. *Come on you old mule,* he thought, *sit on up and scare the shit outta me.* But she didn't.

Taking a deep breath, Ronnie stepped around the kitchen table. He didn't want to look at her lying there on the brown carpet in the living room, but he guessed he really didn't have any choice. If she fell down or something, she might just be unconscious, in which case he'd have to get a doctor right quick. Get a doctor from where? Sanborn? Good fucking luck! Still averting his eyes from the sight on the floor, Ronnie stepped to the side of the archway and flipped on the light switch. The overhead light in the living room came on at once, and what it illuminated made Ronnie piss himself with his hand still on the switch.

From the <u>Grand Rapids Gazette</u>

Grand Rapids, Minnesota

November 19th, 2006

<u>MANHUNT COME TO GRISLEY END</u>

-Nathan Rowley

Four Minnesota men reported missing just after the start of the gun deer season were found Friday. Jacob Larson (54), Eric Larson (19), Steve Ketter (41), and Mike O'toole (48), all hailed from St. Paul. The men were hunting just west of Loon Wing Lake on one-hundred acres of private land owned by Ketter. When the men didn't return from their hunting trip on the 11th, relatives contacted authorities. "We found their truck by their cabin and all their supplies," said Itasca County Sheriff, Ben Carlson, "but the men were nowhere to be found." When the men didn't turn up at the cabin, members of the Sheriff's Department in coordination with the Department of Natural Resources conducted a manhunt to find the missing hunters. The searchers covered as much of the heavily wooded land as they could on foot, but the minimal amount of snow the area has received of late made for poor tracking. On Friday, a Minnesota State Patrol helicopter spotted one of the four men nearly four miles north of Ketter's cabin. Upon further investigation, the other three men were found a short distance away. All four men were dead. Representatives from the Itasca County Sheriff's Department have declined to comment pending completion of the ongoing investigation. However, a senior official at the DNR stated, "It looks like some kind of animal attack."

November 20th, 2006

Grand Rapids, Minnesota

6:02 a.m. CST

        As Ben Carlson pulled into the Itasca County Sheriff's Department parking lot, he felt like someone had slapped him in the back of the head with a nine-iron. The sideshow that started with four missing hunters a little over a week ago had turned into a full-fledged three-ring circus. When the men were reported missing and the hunt began, a reporter from *The Gazette* came along on the search. After a few more days, when the helicopters were called in, reporters from Duluth and Moorhead came in to start asking questions. "Where are they, Sheriff?" they'd ask, and he'd politely reply, "If I knew that, I wouldn't be out here knee-deep in ice looking for them." Last Friday, after the men were found—God rest their souls—a news van from KARE 11 in Minneapolis had been parked outside the station, and newspaper men and women had come from as far as Rochester, Fargo, Mankato and Dubuque to start asking their own questions.

        He left the office last night just after midnight to get a few hours rest before starting over again, and wouldn't you know it, while driving home Ben spotted a white van emblazoned with the red letters, CNN on its side in the parking lot of the Budget Host Inn. *Good God,* he thought, *we've just gone national.*

        Once home, Ben Carlson's headache only intensified. Dawn had picked a hell of a time to start weaning Maggie off the breast. The poor kid was dying to suck but Dawn was sticking to her guns. "The Book says…" was her standard response whenever Ben pleaded with her to try and placate the child. *Dr. Monica Fairchild's Guide to Better Parenting.* The Book. Dr. Fairchild insisted that the child be weaned from the breast at six months. After a week of no sleep, Ben thought that he'd like to take The Book and shove it up the good doctor's ass.

The parking lot of the station was empty except for the overnight dispatcher's squad. Deputy Foster was out on patrol, but he should be back soon along with the rest of the Sheriff's Department. Even before seeing the CNN van, Ben realized that they were all going to need a crash course in media relations and decided to call an early morning meeting. Stepping out of his car into the cold, Ben looked at his watch. He had almost a half an hour before the deputies arrived, and a little less than an hour before the onslaught of the press.

Ben decided twenty minutes ago that if he wasn't sleeping at home, he might as well come in early and organize his thoughts.

Fumbling for the key to the department's back door in the glow of the parking lot light, Ben heard footsteps squeaking in the snow.

"Sheriff Carlson?"

Ben jumped.

"I'm sorry, sir," the voice continued. "I didn't mean to startle you."

The sheriff turned and watched as the tall, bearded man approached. Ben cleared his throat. "I'm in no mood to answer questions," he growled, assuming the man was a reporter.

The stranger reached into his coat pocket and pulled out a wallet. While the man opened it, Ben looked past him and saw a newer sedan parked in the shadows at the edge of the lot.

"My credentials," the stranger said, holding up the wallet.

Ben squinted and looked at the identification. A blue Department of the Interior insignia was printed next to a picture of the man standing before him.

The sheriff sighed. "Department of…? What are you doin' here?"

The man spoke as he put his wallet away. "My name is Jim Door. I need to see the bodies of the hunters."

"What?" Ben couldn't fathom why somebody from the Department of the Interior would need to see the bodies of four dead men at six in the morning.

"I can explain on the way to the morgue, sir."

The sheriff hesitated.

"It's urgent, sir."

November 20th, 2006

Grand Rapids, Minnesota

6:11 a.m. CST

Grand Rapids was deserted as Ben moved his squad car through the snow-covered streets. "So, you're telling me a rogue bear killed those men?"

The stranger nodded in the passenger seat. "That's what we're thinking. We've been following reports out of Canada and now through the northern tier of Minnesota."

Ben turned to look at the man. "More people have been killed?"

"No. It's mostly been dairy cows. A couple of horses."

"Really?"

"Yup. He's been sticking to rural areas, though. Not much for you to worry about here in town. He's kept on the move."

The sheriff was shaking his head. "Yeah, but... how did he get a hold of all four of them hunters?"

"Who knows." The man shrugged. "The bear might have gotten a hold of one of them and the others may have tried to save him."

The fog in Ben's mind caused by the past week of stress and no sleep was beginning to clear as he turned the car off Willow and onto Barker Street. "Why is the Department of the Interior so interested in four hunters killed by a bear?"

In the split second before the man answered, the sheriff had a chance to detect a hint of hesitation. "Well, these days, with all the animal rights groups around, the government has to compile quite a rap sheet before it can kill a man-eater outright. If you don't have your documentation set in stone, if you don't have as much evidence as you would to go to trial against a serial killer, well, these groups can get pretty vicious."

Ben thought about that. It seemed to make sense...

"Why can't you just use the pictures the forensics team took?"

The stranger nodded as if he was expecting this question. "That's because, *officially*, I'm not doing this. I'm not here in Grand Rapids, Minnesota at six in the morning. What the Department does in cases like this is in effect, a PR campaign." The man turned to look directly at the sheriff. "I'm telling you this in confidence, sir, because I think you'll understand."

"Okay." Ben nodded.

"We don't make it obvious to these organizations as to what we're doing. We don't want to give them that much credence. We want to make them think that they are beneath us. What we will do is slowly work with the local and national press, release a few statements through the DNR, and slowly build a case against the marauding bear. In doing so, once we do kill the animal, our case will already be made publicly."

They drove for a few blocks in silence. Ben was nodding his head but he was thinking that the story sounded awful fishy.

"I know this is all a bit strange, sheriff, but let me get a few pictures of the bodies and I'll be out of your hair."

Ben found himself nodding once more as he turned into the Itasca Medical Center's parking lot. Something was wrong about all this, but he couldn't put his finger on what.

"Could I see your identification again, Mr. Door?" Ben asked as they walked towards the hospital entrance.

The man didn't hesitate, pulling out his wallet. "Of course."

As they headed down the stairs to the morgue, the sheriff

studied the ID. It certainly looked official. All the proper names and dates were tattooed all over it. The badge even had a federal hologram over the front that glinted gold-green under the halogens.

"Thank you." Ben handed the badge back.

Once in the morgue, the sheriff quickly told the attendant why they were there. The young man, who was just finishing up his breakfast, didn't look too thrilled about pulling out the bodies, but he wasn't about to argue with the sheriff. Ben stayed by the desk while the stranger followed the attendant over to the bank of refrigerated doors. Ben had seen the bodies up close once, and once was enough. From his vantage point, he watched while the attendant pulled out the appropriate drawers and removed the sheets from the hunters' bodies. Mr. Door pulled a digital camera from the pocket of his coat and began taking pictures of the victims' heads. Each one was obliterated from the ears up. The massive amount of blood lost from the wounds had left the skin of the bodies gray and slack... or was that just the effect of the refrigeration? While his stomach did a momentary loop-de-loop, Ben looked away. He'd seen enough all right.

Mr. Door took only a few pictures of each victim and then returned to where Ben stood. "All right, Sheriff Carlson. I'm all set."

November 20th, 2006

Grand Rapids, Minnesota

6:39 a.m. CST

Once back at the Sheriff's Department, Ben waved the stranger inside. "Come on, you'll have a cup of coffee before you go."

As Ben expected, Door shook his head. "Actually, Sheriff, I've got a long drive ahead of me, so…"

"I won't hear of it. Come on inside." Ben stood with his eyes locked on the stranger's. If the guy made a break for it, that would answer the sheriff's questions. If not, Ben intended to make a phone call to the Department of the Interior, something he was kicking himself for not doing in the first place.

"All right, Sheriff. If you insist."

Ben led the way into the station and to the dispatch desk. The entire staff of the Sheriff's Department was milling about, waiting for the meeting that was supposed to have started ten minutes ago. Ben explained to the others who Mr. Door was, told them to get the man a cup of coffee and said he'd be right back.

The way the small department building was set up, to get out the back door one would have to pass Ben's office. Sitting at his desk, he kept an eye on the hall to make sure Mr. Door wouldn't try to make a getaway. The necessary phone calls took less than five minutes, and in that time, Ben found out exactly what he had thought.

There was no Jim Door at the Department of the Interior. There was no James Door at the Department of the Interior. In fact, there was no one working at the Department of the Interior that had the last name of Door.

Smiling, Ben stood and headed back towards the dispatch area. It was going to feel good to slap the cuffs around the wrists of one of the news people that had been badgering him all week long. This 'Jim Door' obviously wanted an exclusive look at the bodies… well, he was going to get an exclusive look at the inside of a jail cell.

"Where is he?" Ben said, looking around at his deputies. Jim Door was nowhere to be found.

"Where's who?" Foster asked.

"The guy who came in with me!" Ben snapped.

"Oh. He said he forgot something in his car…"

Ben looked over his shoulder. "I didn't see him…"

"He went out the front door," Foster said. "Why? What's the big deal?"

Turning, Ben ran to the back door of the station. When he flung it open and looked across the parking lot, Jim Door's car was gone.

"What's going on?" Deputy Harris asked, coming up behind him.

Ben sighed. For the second time this morning, he felt like he'd been slapped in the back of the head with a nine iron… and it wasn't even seven o'clock yet.

Scott F. Falkner

February 13th, 2007

Catchville, Wisconsin

7:36 p.m. CST

When Seth and Anne walked into the tavern, the Pruitts were sitting where they were before, at the end of the bar closest to the door.

"Well!" Jim Pruitt said, turning on his barstool and lifting up his mug of beer. "Look who made it!"

Seth and Anne nodded to him but said nothing as they walked over and sat midway down the bar. Skip was still on his stool. To his left were the guys from the gas station, the clerk and the old guy he'd called Dizzy.

"What can I get for you, Mr. and Mrs. Landon?" Maggie asked.

"Pitcher of beer, Maggie," Seth said. "Please."

The bartender nodded and started to pour.

"This is probably going to be a slow night I'd guess?" Seth said, trying to make conversation.

Maggie nodded and said without turning, "Yup. Usually Fridays are pretty good too. I run some better specials down here than they do at the saloons up in Sanborn, so I get quite a bit of business from up there."

"The fine citizens of Catchville must be staying in tonight as well," Seth said.

Maggie stopped filling the pitcher and looked up and down the bar. "Nope. Except for Mrs. Meadows, they're all here."

Seth leaned forward and looked down the bar. "Wait a

minute..."

The bartender smiled. "That's right. Less, Dizzy, Mrs. Meadows, my niece and myself are it. Catchville ain't exactly a metropolis, Mr. Landon. We're more of... well, an outpost of sorts. Kind of a rest stop between Highway 53 and Sanborn." She finished getting their beer while she spoke and put the pitcher and glasses down in front of them.

"Wow," Anne said. "I had no idea that it was *that* small."

"Yup. We're just a little speck up here in the big old Wisconsin wilderness."

February 13th, 2007

Catchville, Wisconsin

7:58 p.m. CST

When the door to the bar burst open, Seth and Anne had just refilled their glasses.

"Maggie!" Ronnie Eaves screamed from the doorway. "Maggie!"

Everyone in the bar turned to look. Ronnie was dusted with snow from head to foot and his eyes were bulging with fear. He moved across the bar as his chest heaved for breath. Wherever Ronnie had come from, he'd done it at a run.

"What are you yelling about, Ronnie?" Maggie said from behind the bar.

"Maggie!" he screamed again. Seth thought the man looked like he was in shock. He and Anne stood up and aside so that the man could come right up to the bar.

"What is it, Ron?" Skip asked.

"Mrs. Meadows!" he shrieked between gasps for air.

"What?" Maggie's own voice now sounded urgent. "What's happened to Mrs. Meadows?"

"Dead!" Ronnie yelped. He placed both hands on the bar and leaned into it.

"Now, catch your breath, Ronnie," Maggie was saying from behind the bar. "Get a hold of yourself."

His breathing started to slow down. "Mrs. Meadows is dead. I seen her."

Maggie sighed. "The poor old dear," she muttered. "These

damn winters finally caught up with her."

Ronnie shook his head furiously back and forth. "No. No, I think she was shot!"

The young man's words hung like a shadow over the bar.

"Now hang on a second," Maggie put her hand up, "Ronnie, what exactly did you see?"

More heaving breaths prompted Skip to step forward and hold out his beer glass to Ronnie. He took it, though his hand was shaking so badly that much of it spilled over the rim as he brought it to his lips and drained it. The beer seemed to soothe him a bit, and after a few seconds he spoke.

"When I got there the kitchen door was open. I went inside. She was on the living room floor..." They all watched as the memory of what Ronnie saw caught up with him. He clenched his teeth and slammed his eyes shut, but the tears still came. "Oh shit..."

"It's all right, Ron," Maggie said, her voice comforting. "What did you see?"

Ronnie opened up his eyes. His now-wet cheeks reflected the soft light from above the bar. "Someone blew her face clean off."

February 13th, 2007

Catchville, Wisconsin

8:04 p.m. CST

Seth and Anne backed away from the bar as Skip and Dizzy and the guy from the gas station all started pressing Ronnie for more details about Mrs. Meadows. The door to the kitchen swung open and Audrey came out looking around for an explanation to all the shouting only minutes earlier. Jim and Nancy Pruitt were talking animatedly between themselves, and Seth could almost see the gears in Mr. Pruitt's head working; he was thinking of taking his wife and getting the hell out of Catchville. Anne looked at Maggie. The bartender was silently biting her lip behind the bar. It was clear that she was trying to sort out all of the details of the last few minutes. Then, all at once, she glanced up at Anne and then at the room.

"Listen up." Everyone was silent at once. "Everyone keep calm. We don't know what's happened."

"What's going on, Aunt Maggie?" Audrey asked, the fear readable on her features.

For the moment, Maggie ignored her. "Skip?"

He looked in her direction.

"Please go lock the front door." As Skip and the bar matron shared a short stare, the weight of Maggie's words fell heavily on the bar. If Maggie wanted the door locked, it gave credence to the idea that someone—someone dangerous—was out in the cold that needed to be guarded against.

"Aunt Maggie?"

"Audrey, please go and make sure the back door is locked."

The girl bit her lip before turning and heading back into the kitchen.

"Everyone else stay calm," Maggie said to the bar at large. "I'm sure there's an explanation for all this. I'm calling the police up in Sanborn and we'll all just sit tight until they tell us what to do."

Anne saw that everyone in the bar was vaguely nodding their heads in unison. That was the logical conclusion—call the cops.

Maggie walked to the wall near the kitchen doors where the phone was attached and picked it up. Everyone was on pins and needles as Maggie stood with the phone to her ear. She tapped the phone clicker twice with her finger and then hung it up. Shaking her head, she turned around.

"The phone's dead."

Skip shrugged walking back up to the bar. "In this weather, you shouldn't be surprised."

A new round of murmurs started. "My cell won't work!" Nancy Pruitt exclaimed, looking at the phone in her hand.

"That's not surprising," the gas station clerk said. "This whole valley is a dead zone for them portable phones. They never seem to work around here."

Ronnie leaned against the bar and started shaking his head. "Oh my God! Oh my God!"

"Everybody shut up!" Maggie yelled.

In the silence that followed, everyone listened to the wind whipping against the walls of the tavern.

"I've got the radio over at the station," Less finally said. "As long as the power ain't out, we can use that."

"Are you crazy?" Ronnie said, his voice cracking between every word. "Don't you get it Lester? There's a goddamn murderer out there! Somebody shot her! Don't you get it you old coot?" He shook his fists when he spoke.

"Settle down," Maggie's voice was calm. "Audrey, get him some coffee." She turned back to Less. "The land lines are out. Everybody knows that a cell phone doesn't have a chicken's chance in hell of working here in the valley. But I don't think it's such a good idea to go over to the station, Less. I think we oughtta stay put for the time being."

"For how long?" Jim asked. "You expect us to just sit here all night buying your booze?"

Maggie's jaw was set as she turned to look at the man. "What I think we ought to do, Mr. Pruitt, is not lose our heads. We have no information besides the account of a man three-sheets to the wind. We can't start jumping to conclusions."

"You don't believe me, Maggie?" Ronnie was genuinely hurt.

"No. I believe you, Ronnie. I believe you saw something, but until we know what that something is we can't start going off half-cocked."

There was some more discussion and debate, but Seth was distracted by Anne pulling on his arm. He followed as she gently led him to the nearest booth. "What is it?" he whispered when they sat.

"I have to tell you, Seth, that I'm a bit frightened." She smiled at the preciseness of her own statement. "What do you think we should do?"

He thought for a moment. "I think Maggie's right. I think we should stay put until the police can be called. It'll probably turn out that the lady had a heart attack and hit her head on a table. That Ronnie guy is so drunk he probably doesn't know what he saw."

"Yeah." Anne nodded. "You're probably right."

"There's no harm in me goin' over to the station and using

the radio!" Less pulled on his jacket as he rounded the bar.

"Less!" Maggie raised her own voice. The two of them exchanged a long stare. The look of determination in Less' eyes made it clear that he intended to go out whether anyone in the bar thought it was a good idea or not. "Just hang on a second," Maggie finally said before she disappeared into the kitchen. Presently she came back through the steel doors carrying a shotgun. As everyone watched in silence, the woman cracked the gun open, checked the contents of the barrels, and closed it back up. She walked around the edge of the bar and handed it to Less.

"Don't go shootin' anyone. There's two shells in there, but... well, just use it to scare somebody... if you have to. You hear me?"

Less nodded his head but Seth thought he saw the man's hands shaking as he took the shotgun.

February 13th, 2007

Catchville, Wisconsin

8:13 p.m. CST

Less Huggard had lived in Catchville, Wisconsin for going on nineteen years. He'd moved down from Ashland, where he was born and raised, on a tip from a friend. A gas station was for sale in an out of the way town that saw lots of thru-traffic. For Less, it sounded like a gold mine selling dirt-cheap. When he came to Catchville for the first time he'd been shocked to find that the place was even categorized as a town. He had serious misgivings about buying the place, but, after talking to the then owner, he'd sat in his Oldsmobile in the station parking lot and watched how many cars stopped in for gas on that August afternoon. After the nineteenth car rolled up to the gas pump in the span of an hour, Less called his banker and made the deal.

Everything was fine at first, that was, until winter set in. How many days had he sat behind the counter looking out at the empty parking lot wondering how the hell a man who'd grown up in Wisconsin could have forgotten about the savage northern Wisconsin winters? It became clear that Less would have to make a living on all the money he made between April and early September, which wasn't what he'd hoped to be making when he came to Catchville. Oh, he made ends meet near enough, the small house he bought a hundred feet or so from the station wasn't all that expensive, but it was clear that he wasn't ever going to get far enough ahead for an early retirement.

Less' eyes batted back and forth as he walked to the edge of Maggie's parking lot. The wind had really picked up now, blowing snow into drifts two feet high in some places. Shivering, Less scolded himself for not wearing an extra flannel or sweater underneath his coat. *But that's not it*, he told himself. *You know damn well that that's not the reason you're shivering. You're shivering because there might be someone else out here who's got a gun. You're shivering because despite how drunk Ronnie is, Mrs. Meadows might just have really been shot in the head by someone, and that same someone might be out here on the street.*

He jogged diagonally across the highway in the general direction of the gas station. Where was the damn light? Usually, even in the toughest snow, you could see the station's light from the end of Maggie's parking lot. This blizzard was a whopper, and it didn't show any signs of letting up.

Less' boots kicked through a drift that came up to his knees. *Careful now*, he told himself, gripping the shotgun so that it was parallel to his chest, *with these drifts you've got to pay attention to where you're going. If you get off of the edge of the road, you'll be in a shit-heap of trouble.*

After jogging another ten or fifteen yards along the highway, Less could make out the barest glimmer of the Amoco sign. *Gods be praised!* Less thought briefly about holding the gun with one hand and fishing the keys to the station out of his pocket with the other, but then decided against it. The gun felt reassuring in his hands and besides, it'd be a pisser to fumble and drop the keys here in the dark. *I'll wait until I get under the light, so I can see what I'm doing.*

A strong gust of wind blew into Less' face making him raise up his arms and stop. It only took a moment for the gust to pass, but in that moment Less felt extremely vulnerable. He looked about himself, as much as the snow allowed, and all at once had the feeling that he was being watched.

"Knock it off!" he told himself. "You're just givin' yourself the creeps." That was easy enough to think, and yet, as he continued at a hurried pace towards the station, Less Huggard kept glancing over his shoulders. When he reached the door he turned and backed up all the way against the glass. Holding the gun over his shoulder with one hand, he pulled the keys out of his pocket with his other. Less felt the blood pumping through his temples as he let himself into the station and pulled the glass door shut behind him. He stood there for a few moments, his nose pressed against the door, his breath steaming it up as he searched the parking lot for any sign of movement.

"What a scaredy-cat," he said out loud, smiling. But before heading to the office in the back, Less reached out and locked the door. "I guess being a scaredy-cat can't be all bad." He was halfway to the counter to turn on the overhead lights when he second-guessed himself. Right now the only lights on in the store were the dim lamps above the cigarette racks and the red EXIT sign over the door in the back. If he turned on the fluorescents, someone would *definitely* know that he was in the store.

That sinister thought flashed back through his head; What if someone really had shot Old Lady Meadows? What if that someone was still in town? What if that someone still had an itchy trigger finger? Why take chances?

Less walked down the aisle in the dim light through the center of the store. There, he fumbled again with his keys and unlocked the door that was marked EMPLOYEES ONLY. Beyond the door lay a hallway ending in the rear exit. On the left side of the hall were two more doors that led to the cold and general storage areas. To the right was the office. This door wasn't locked, and as there were no windows to the outside Less flicked on the overhead lights and leaned the shotgun against the doorjamb.

The radio sat on top of a table on the left side of the office, across from his desk on the right. Less went to it at once and felt for the power switch on the side.

At the exact same moment Less pushed the switch, he heard the crash of glass from out in the store.

Less Huggard froze. *"Shit!"* he hissed through his teeth. He held his breath and listened, but the only thing audible in the office was the hum of the overhead lights and the static from the radio. Less reached out, turned the volume on the radio all the way down, and stepped over to pick up the shotgun.

Rationalization tried to take over the forefront of his mind; *the wind just caught a scrap of wood or something and flung it into one of the windows... that's all you heard.*

The rear part of his mind shook its head at that thought. Somebody had broken into the station.

Less put his ear to the inside of the office door and listened. Why hadn't he stayed at the bar? Why had he been so goddamned adamant about going to the station and calling the police on the radio? Who was he trying to impress?

He took a deep breath. *Well, Jackass, you got yourself into this mess so now you'd better get yourself out.* Less swallowed, clenched his dentures and gripped the shotgun with his right hand. Slowly, he turned the knob on the office door and pulled it open. Less backed up and raised the rifle to his shoulder. The hall was dark except for the red light cast by the EXIT sign above the back door.

Less edged out into the hallway. He hadn't heard anyone opening the door to the back hall, so he assumed that whoever was in the station was still up front.

His breath came in quick, big gasps now. He tried to calm himself by holding back the urgency of the breaths, but it didn't work. Holding back the breaths only made the next one he took become that much larger. What the hell was going on? Less couldn't seem to get enough air! He felt like he was suffocating!

"That's enough!" he told himself in a sub-whisper. "You're fine." *You're standing in the back hall of the gas station like you've done a thousand times before, the only difference is that this time you're in the dark, you're holding a shotgun and there may very well be an armed killer on the other side of the door you're facing.* "Jesus!"

He was almost to the door when his courage gave. If he'd wanted to, he could've reached out and grabbed the doorknob, but that was never really in the cards. *Hell, you're no hero*, he told himself. *Why should you be the one to take this lunatic on? Why should you risk your stinkin' neck?*

"Nope," Less whispered. "Not for me." He backed away from the door. He was going to back up all the way to the rear exit and go ahead and take it outside. Then he was going to run as hard as his old heart could manage back to Maggie's. They might tease him when he got there. They might tell him...

WHAM!

The door in front of Less flew open. By the time his fingers squeezed the trigger of the shotgun—purely by reflex—the gun had already been knocked aside. It all happened so fast! The main thing that registered in Less Huggard's brain were the eyes of the thing; they were aware eyes, frantic eyes, but they were fogged over with some sort of bluish film that looked purple in the red light of the hallway. The thing hit him with incredible force and he found himself on his back looking up at it. In an instant a smell rained down on him, a putrid smell of fecal death. Less' senses recoiled and he felt his chest heave as his stomach contracted. But he wouldn't get a chance to vomit. The hand that clutched at his neck was so cold he could feel the chill through his layers of clothing. The other hand, white, and seeming to be made of nothing but bone and muscle was slapped across his face, pinning his head to the tiled floor.

Less Huggard tried to scream, but he didn't have a last scream in him. Through the index and middle finger of the thing on top of him, he caught a glimpse of the widening mouth, its bloodless lips flush up against its teeth. Before Less had a chance to process what the thing intended to do, he felt several sharp points tear into the top of his forehead. He had a split second to liken the feeling to that of a headache and then... nothing.

From the <u>Superior Sentinel</u>

Superior, Wisconsin

December 28th, 2006

HITCHHIKERS MAULED

-Jessica Marbhel

Two unidentified hitchhikers were found dead yesterday on Highway W, two miles south of Oliver. The victims were described by police as 'two individuals, a man and a woman, both in their twenties.' Oliver resident, Mary Hess, told the *Sentinel* she saw the victims. "I told the police I saw them on my way to work yesterday morning," Hess stated. A clerk at the Superior Citgo, Hess said, "I noticed them because I thought it was rather strange to see hitchhikers in December. They looked like they were freezing. I almost stopped to pick them up, but I didn't. Now I kind of wished that I had." Early reports from the Douglas County Coroner's Office indicate that the victims died of massive head wounds. When this reporter inquired as to the safety of the public at large, Douglas County Sheriff's Department Public Relations Officer Jeanie Black said, "Preliminary reports from the coroner indicate that it was a freak animal attack. Of course, we won't know until the final report is issued, but for now we feel that there's no need to put the public on alert." A representative from the State Forensics Office in Madison has been summoned to try and determine the identities of the two victims.

February 13th, 2007

Catchville, Wisconsin

8:31 p.m. CST

The process of waiting became an uneasy event for everyone in Maggie's bar. Ronnie Eaves had retreated to one of the booths where he sat gazing into his cup of coffee. Skip had downed one beer, and after some consideration, one more before moving over to the jukebox and picking out a few Golden Oldies. Dizzy Vaughn sat on his barstool, sipping his beer and chain-smoking while staring at himself in the long mirror behind the bar. Audrey found solace from the nervous tension by cleaning whatever she could; she'd washed and rinsed every glass in the place, and now had moved on to sweeping up the kitchen floor. Jim and Nancy Pruitt were both a ball of nervous tension. Nancy kept holding her cell phone at arm's length looking for a signal and Jim kept asking anyone who would listen about Mrs. Meadows and how long the phone lines usually took to get fixed during a storm. Maggie had endured these questions for a while, but after fifteen minutes she'd finally told him that she didn't have the answers he was looking for. "I just don't know, Mr. Pruitt. I know as much as you do." That had shut him up for a few minutes until he started whispering to his wife. Maggie had gone over and checked the phone twice now, knowing both times that it was futile. The phone company wasn't crazy enough to head out tonight in the storm to fix the lines. If they did, odds were that they'd just go down again by morning and they'd have to start all over again.

Maggie didn't like this situation at all. She was used to normality and routine, it was something she enjoyed after a fashion, but she hadn't realized just how much she'd come to depend on that normality over the years. Now that something utterly strange might have happened in Catchville, Maggie didn't know what to do with herself. But that was the problem, wasn't it? No one knew if something strange had happened. Maggie had been through umpteen different variations on what might have happened to Mrs. Meadows in her mind, but without checking on the poor old woman herself, Maggie couldn't be sure of any of them. Less will be back soon, she kept telling herself. The police will tell Less what to do and then he'll tell us and then we'll do it, simple as that. Only… Maggie looked at her watch. Less should've been back by now. Of course, his delay could be explained in a dozen different ways; perhaps when he radioed the police they told him to stay put until they arrived. That led to another question: did the police in Sanborn have the equipment to get to Catchville? Did they have a snow cat or some such that they'd rush on down in? Maggie didn't think so. Perhaps Less ran over to his house after he went to the gas station. It would be a stupid thing to do, but she wouldn't put it past him. So now what? Now she would wait.

"This is getting old." Anne looked at her watch. "I hope we don't have to spend the whole night here."

The entire ordeal of waiting was starting to grind on Seth's nerves too, so much so that he felt the urge to blame Anne for wanting to come to Catchville in the first place. But that wasn't right. This situation wasn't Anne's fault to be sure. The two of them had ordered another pitcher of beer but so far neither one had worked through more than half a glass.

"I know," Seth finally said.

All at once the lights in the bar went out.

A shadow of silence accompanied the dark. The jukebox, from which Dean Martin had just been crooning *Volare*, went dead.

"Everyone stay put. I'll get some lights." It was Maggie's voice. Seth thought that if the woman ever decided to move to a larger town, she'd be a prime candidate for mayor; she was born to be in charge.

"You all right, babe?" Seth whispered, reaching out across the table. Anne's hands grasped his at once.

"Yeah."

Maggie came back out of the kitchen carrying two large kerosene lamps and a flashlight. She sat one lamp on the bar and handed the other to Skip to put on the pool table in the center of the room. Soon the tavern became light enough for everyone to see what they were doing.

Maggie didn't want to say anything, at least not yet. But they were all now going to be faced with another dilemma. The bar had no generator. It was going to get cold soon, uncomfortably cold. Eventually they'd all have to move over to the hotel where the generator would've kicked in to heat the first floor. But there was no point in telling them that now. There was enough nervousness in the building as it was.

Maggie watched as Skip walked back up to the end of the bar and started towards her.

"Mags?" he whispered, though in the total silence it was hard not to hear him.

She raised her eyebrows.

"I think it's time I go find out what's keeping Less."

Blowing air through puckered lips, Maggie nodded. "I guess so. But you're not gonna go alone." She turned to grab her coat from the hook on the wall.

"No, Maggie," Skip said, his voice raising a bit. "You stay here. These people need you in the bar."

She turned back to him. "You're not going alone," she repeated.

Skip nodded. "All right. I'll take..." He was going to say "Ronnie", but as he looked out over the room, past the pool table to where Ronnie sat in the booth, Skip knew that his friend was too shaken up to be going anywhere. Dizzy was too old. If there was someone out there in the snowy dark, Dizzy would become more of a hindrance than a help.

Skip looked at Mr. Pruitt. Nope. Skip had only been acquainted with the man for a few hours, but he didn't trust him any farther than he could throw him. Rounding the end of the bar, Skip crossed the room.

"Mr. Landon?"

Seth looked at his wife and then back up at Skip. "I guess if I'm going to be running around in the dark with you, you can call me Seth."

Skip nodded and headed back up to the bar.

"Are you sure about this?" Anne said, squeezing Seth's hand.

He forced a grin. "You said you didn't want to spend all night here…"

Anne didn't return his smile.

Seth looked up at the bar and saw Maggie hand two large knives to Skip. "Just in case," she said.

"I'm no hero." Seth looked back to Anne. "I'll run before I have to stab anyone."

He stood up and began to put on his coat and gloves. Anne stood with him. "Be careful."

Seth pulled on his hat. "You don't have to tell me twice."

"Ready?" Skip asked, approaching them. He held out one of the knives, handle first, and gave it to Seth.

"Uh, I think so." He saw the look of worry on Anne's face and quickly nodded. "Yeah. Yeah, I'm ready. We'll be fine, Sweetie."

She nodded but the terror remained in her eyes. "'Love you," she said, kissing him. He kissed her back before pulling away.

"Love you too. See you in a bit."

February 13th, 2007

Catchville, Wisconsin

8:42 p.m. CST

Seth fell in step behind Skip as they moved across the parking lot. The storm hadn't subsided a jot. The air was awash with fat snowflakes that stuck to their clothing. Shielding his eyes, Seth scanned the ground about them but could see no sign of the gas station owner's footprints. Of course, that was no real surprise; the blizzard's fury was such that tracks in the snow wouldn't last for more than a few minutes.

Seth looked back up and realized he'd meandered a few yards to the right of Skip while looking down at the snow. He quickly reordered his course and made a mental note to keep track of the other man at all times. In this weather it wouldn't take much more than ten seconds to lose the light of Skip's flashlight.

"There's the road."

Seth looked ahead. To his eyes, he couldn't see much of a difference between the snow-packed surface Skip pointed to and the snow-packed surface they were now on.

The two men worked their way down the center of the highway, their boots rhythmically slashing through the snowdrifts. Seth could feel his heart pounding in his chest and though he glanced up often to see what sort of progress they were making, he could see no farther in the darkness than the reach of Skip's flashlight beam.

A thought occurred to Seth as they trudged along; his fear had vanished.

The idea that someone had broken into an old lady's house and shot her in the head, the idea that that someone was still out here—and possibly on a murderous rampage—had really taken its toll on Seth's imagination over the last hour or so. But now, out in the midst of the blizzard and being unable to see more than a dozen yards in any direction, the thought of anyone being able to see well enough to do them any harm seemed ludicrous.

"Look out!"

Seth stopped. Skip was pointing the flashlight at the gas pump in front of the Amoco station. Seth couldn't believe that they were actually in the station's lot. He didn't even realize they'd left the road.

Skip shined his light on the front door of the building. "Holy shit."

Seth's fear came back like a razor sharp boomerang. Ahead of them, less than a dozen feet from where they stood, they saw the broken store window. Shattered glass reflected off of the flashlight beam to the right of the gas station's door.

Not taking his eyes off of the broken glass, Seth spoke. "Well Skip… what do you think?"

In his peripheral vision, Seth saw the older man shrug.

"I'll tell you what I don't think," Skip said, "I don't think Less forgot his keys and decided to break into his own place."

Seth nodded. He didn't think that the station owner had broken his own window either. "What do we do?"

For several, cloudy breaths, Skip remained silent. Finally, he sighed. "I suppose we oughtta go in and find out what happened."

"Yeah… I suppose." Though the agreement had been made, neither man moved for several long moments.

"Why don't we go around back and see what we can see?" Skip finally said. Seth looked up at him and smiled. Hell yeah, anything to put off going in that damned gas station was fine by him.

Nothing seemed to be amiss as Seth followed Skip around the side of the building. Drifts as high as three to four feet had amassed at the wall of the gas station, and the two men gave them a wide berth. There were no windows here, so neither of them could get a glimpse of any movement from within.

They didn't see the open rear door of the gas station right away. Skip had his flashlight pointed at the ground in front of them, looking for any sign of footprints or other marks. When he did see the open door, however, he stopped so quickly that Seth ran right into him.

"What...?" Seth started to ask a question but Skip held up his hand. Seth got the point. He took a quiet sidestep to see past the older man. The back door, the door that had no handle on its outside, the door that was only to be used in case of an emergency, was wide open. Someone had pushed it open from the inside and the deep snow had prevented it from closing.

Leaning very close to Skip—far closer than he ever thought he would—Seth whispered in the older man's ear. "What do we do?"

Skip answered not with words but with a few tentative steps forward. Seth wanted to cry out, to ask the guy what the hell he thought he was doing, but then he got a hold of himself. If the window in the front of the store was crashed in, and this door was wide open in the back, this door with no handle on the outside... well, then logic dictated that someone had broken in the front and left via the back.

Didn't it?

Seth wasn't so sure. He sighed, gripped his knife a bit tighter, and started to follow. Skip was halfway to the door now along the rear wall of the gas station. He was holding his knife out at his side, its tip pointed down. Seth bit his lip as he watched the older man look around the corner. Skip held up the hand holding the knife a bit higher as he used his other to point the flashlight into the building.

"Oh…" Skip moaned, or at least Seth thought he heard Skip moan. Between the stocking cap pulled tight over his ears and the thrumming of the wind it was difficult to discern anything. However, when Skip turned back to look at him, the expression on the guy's face said that he probably *had* moaned.

"Jesus on a biscuit!" Skip hissed and stepped back from the doorway. He handed Seth the flashlight and nodded to the door.

Seth took it and suddenly felt like there was a gumball lodged in his throat. Stepping up to the edge of the entrance, he clenched his knife in his right hand, held the flashlight in his left and looked around the corner. He saw at once that this door led to a hallway that probably came out in the back of the store. There were a few doors off of the hall, but on the floor… Seth clenched his teeth. Lying on the floor in a pool of red was who Seth assumed to be Less. Seth could only assume it was the gas station owner as the top of his head was gone.

January 16th, 2007

Barnes, Wisconsin

5:15 p.m. CST

Tully Sanford put down his pencil and stared at the ledger. There were no two ways about it, the ranch was in the red, and there was no amount of number crunching that was going to make the red turn black. Oh, they'd survive, but it was going to be rough ride until spring. Once more, Tully damned himself for buying such a lavish present for his girl. They didn't have the money for it, and now Sheila's colt was dead. Killed. How could anyone be so cruel?

A pair of headlights shined through his office window. Were Mary and Sheila coming back early? Who else would be driving in at this time of day?

Tully stood up, walked out of the office and through the kitchen. From the window above the sink he saw that it wasn't Sheila. The dark sedan passed the barn and parked in driveway. Who the hell was this? Another creditor from the bank?

A tall, bearded man wearing a thick winter coat stepped out of the car and started for the house.

"Mr. Sanford?" the man said as Tully opened the front door.

"Yes…?" Tully answered carefully.

"My name is Dave Smith. I breed Arabians. I was just passing through town and I stopped to eat at the diner. One of the waitresses was speaking of the tragedy that you experienced out here and I just felt like I should stop by."

Whatever Tully was expecting to hear from the man, this certainly wasn't it. "Oh?" was all he could think of to say.

The stranger continued. "I wanted to express my sympathies… and perhaps offer some assistance."

"Oh," Tully said again while scratching his chin. "Assistance?"

"Well, if I can be honest with you, Mr. Sanford, a lot of times law enforcement doesn't take these crimes as seriously as they should. A few years back a group of duck hunters decided to take target practice on a pair of my mares at my ranch in Colorado. Suffice to say, I had to collect my own evidence, put two and two together and bring the culprits to the courthouse at the end of my own lasso."

Tully's eyes grew wide. Oh how he'd like to find the psycho that killed Sheila's colt and deal out some justice of his own.

The stranger looked at his watch. "But unfortunately, my time is short. If I'm to help you, we've got to be quick about it. I need a look at your horse. What do you say, Mr. Sanford?"

Tully was nothing short of tongue-tied. Sure, Sheriff Norton hadn't seemed gung-ho about finding the maniac that had killed Sheila's colt when he'd come over this morning, but how could this guy help him…

"Mr. Sanford?"

Tully shook his head. What the hell? It couldn't hurt. He stuck out his hand and shook the stranger's. "Call me Tully."

January 16th, 2007

Barnes, Wisconsin

5:21 p.m. CST

As they walked around the side of the barn, the stranger quizzed Tully on the death of his colt.

"Well, I ran into town last night, I guess it was about a quarter to five when I left. As my wife and daughter have been gone for the last week I thought I'd go down to the A&W and get myself a decent meal. I'm afraid I'm not so good at cooking for myself."

Dave Smith nodded, but by the look in his eyes Tully could tell that the man was in no mood for chitchat.

"I bought the colt earlier this week from Dick Harrigan. You know him?"

Dave Smith shook his head.

"Oh. Well, Dick's got a nice size spread just the other side of Drummond. Things have been kinda tight this season and I was feeling a bit down in the mouth about not getting my Sheila a really good Christmas present. Her and her mother are over to my mother-in-law's for a spell—they're due back on Monday—so I thought I'd go ahead and splurge on a colt for my girl." Tully took a deep breath as they rounded the barn and headed along its back side. He wiped his eye and then moved his hand up to adjust his hat so the stranger wouldn't think he was crying. Damn! Sheila was gonna be devastated by the news!

"God knows we don't got the money, but I figured if we stretched things a bit..." Tully glanced at the stranger and saw that look in his eye again; that look that said, *Get on with it.* "Ever since I got the horse it's run the fence line along the drive in the evenings.

I came home from town about quarter of six and noticed that she wasn't anywhere in the front pasture. Well, I came around back and..."

Tully hadn't really thought on what he'd seen when he'd gotten home last evening. Even lying in bed last night he dismissed the memory of the image from his mind. He did think of how sad Sheila would be when she found out that the colt Tully had told her about on the phone was dead. He did think about how angry Mary was going to be when she found out how much money he spent on the damn thing. But he hadn't thought about how the horse was killed because it was just too awful.

A single, yellow bulb hung from a rusted fixture above the rear barn door. Just out of its glow—some twelve yards out into the pasture—lay the canvas-covered hump.

"That it?" Dave Smith asked.

Tully nodded.

The two men walked across the thin crusting of snow. Their boots crunching on the ice were the only sounds in the pasture and Tully found the usually peaceful silence now eerie.

"I cuh-covered it up last night," Tully stuttered.

If the stranger heard him he gave no indication. Tully stopped a full ten feet away from the tarp. He had no inclination to get any closer. Even in the dim light he could already see the red stains in the snow around the edge of the tarp. For the briefest of moments the memory of what he saw yesterday flashed through his mind and Tully's stomach lurched. He looked away, toward the woods, and blew out three quick, cloudy breaths.

It took a moment to process what he was seeing when Tully turned back. Dave Smith was crouching near the edge of the tarp. He'd taken off his winter gloves and was replacing them with latex ones from his pocket.

"Did you move her at all, Tully?" the stranger asked without looking up.

Tully was thinking to himself that the man had certainly come prepared. "No. No I didn't."

Smith pointed around the edges of the tarp. "Then these footprints, these ones in the red, they were here when you found her?"

Nodding, Tully put his hands on his hips.

The frozen, plastic tarp made a horrific ripping sound as the stranger pulled it up off of the horse. Tully found that his eyes were fixed on the colt lying on its side. The wound the killer had caused exposed the entire brain cavity of the animal. Tendrils and lumps of red flesh that had been warm enough to steam last night were now gray and rigid.

The stranger leaned down and examined the head wound. Then, as Tully watched, the man took a small case from his jacket pocket, and from the case he removed a camera.

Not knowing what to say or think, Tully stayed silent as the stranger snapped off pictures of the dead horse and the surrounding area. A few minutes later Dave Smith stopped, and stood looking to the northwest. The stranger was following the line of the footprints, same as Tully had done after he found the horse.

"What's out there?" Smith asked without turning.

Tully shrugged. "Nothing but woods and more woods. Kelly Lake is up there a spell, but after that you get into the national forest, and… like I said, more woods."

Finally Smith turned back. "Any roads through the forest?"

"Not really. You can't log it. You can't hunt it. Why the hell would anybody go there?"

At that, the stranger smiled and slipped his camera and case back into his pocket. While Smith was taking off the latex gloves, Tully finally got up the nerve to ask what was on his mind.

"You're not really a horse owner, are you Mr. Smith?"

The stranger stuffed the used gloves into another pocket and pulled on his winter ones. Finally, he looked up at Tully. "Mr. Sanford, I'll find out who did this. I'll bring him to justice, but I'm afraid you'll never hear about it."

Tully eyed the stranger closely. "Smith ain't even your name, is it?"

The stranger pulled the tarp back over the horse and then led the way around the barn. "When's animal disposal come?" the man asked.

Tully, still on edge, took a moment to answer. "I called them this morning and he said he'd come on Monday."

They said nothing else until they were in front of the barn and standing next to the dark blue sedan.

"When's your wife and daughter get back, Mr. Sanford?" the stranger asked as he pulled his wallet from his back pocket. While Tully watched suspiciously, the man began to sort through the wallet's contents.

"Uh, next week. You want to tell me who you are and what you're doing here?"

The stranger smiled as he began to pull money from the wallet. After a moment, he handed a wad of bills across the hood of the car to Tully.

"What's this for?"

"Maybe it'll be enough that you're daughter will never have to know what happened to that horse." The man opened his car door. "I wish I could give you more but it's all I can spare at the moment. Thank you, Mr. Sanford."

Tully didn't realize his mouth was wide open until the stranger's car was halfway down the drive. He looked down at the money in his hand. There were ten bills in the wad, and they were all hundreds.

For weeks to come, Tully Sanford often looked down at

the end of the driveway and wondered who the man that called himself Dave Smith really was.

February 13th, 2007

Catchville, Wisconsin

8:56 p.m. CST

As soon as Skip and Seth had left Maggie's Tavern, Anne moved up to sit at the bar. It was far too lonely—not to mention, spooky—sitting alone in the booth. Maggie and Audrey were standing on the other side of rail, Jim and Nancy Pruitt were sitting to Anne's right, and the old man, Dizzy, was sitting to her left sucking on yet another cigarette. Ronnie Eaves was apparently passed out in his booth. His head buried in his arm like a sleeping bird, Ronnie hadn't moved for at least fifteen minutes.

"Where are they?" Jim asked as Maggie started to hand out coffee cups. Dizzy waved his cup off as he still had half a glass of beer sitting in front of him on the bar.

Though Anne had laughed at Jim Pruitt when she and Seth were in their hotel room, now she didn't find him funny at all. Five minutes after Seth and Skip left, Pruitt had started wondering how long it'd take before they got back. Five minutes later he'd started wondering aloud where they were and what might have happened to them. Anne didn't want to think about what might have happened to them because the only scenarios she could come up with in her imagination were too terrible.

"It's going to take some time," Maggie said, pouring coffee into Anne's cup. "Skip's not going to do any rushing in this weather, it'd be too easy to get lost in the dark."

Though the woman's comment was intended to alleviate Anne's fears, it did just the opposite.

Maggie continued. "Once they get over to the station, if Less isn't there Skip will go ahead and call the police on the radio himself."

Nancy Pruitt interrupted. "What if the gas station's locked? How are they going to get in?"

The bartender shot the woman a look laced with pure venom. "Skip will figure something out. I know Skip, and if he's gotta, he'll break a window to get into the station."

"It's almost nine o'clock," Jim said, looking once more at his watch.

To Anne's left, Dizzy Vaughn cleared his throat. "I think we all know what time it is, mister. Why don't you keep your minute-by-minute reports to yourself."

Anne sipped her coffee. It was already lukewarm, as it had started to cool in the pot when the power went out. Anne wasn't sure, but she thought that the temperature in the bar had already dropped by ten degrees. That made her wonder just how cold it was outside.

"Look," Jim's voice got louder, "we've got one dead woman and three missing men out there! If my mentioning the time has got you flustered old man…"

Anne saw Maggie's mouth opening to intercede when there was a hard knock at the front door of the tavern.

For a split second they all just sat in silence. Then, as realization kicked in, Anne turned, got off of her barstool and headed for the front door.

"Make sure it's them!" Nancy Pruitt called after her, but Anne didn't hear. She rushed to the door, flipped the lock and opened it up.

A burst of snow accompanied Skip and Seth as they came barreling through the door. Anne was instantly relieved to see her husband unharmed. However, when she saw the wide, vacant look in his eyes and the shotgun slung over Skip's shoulder, that relief became tempered with a fair amount of apprehension.

"Seth!" She grabbed him with both arms and pulled his

cold body against hers. "Seth, what happened?"

Her husband lifted his head and looked into her eyes. Anne saw that his face was a hard white, and from his expression she didn't think it was white from the cold. "What happened?"

Seth's mouth parted only slightly when he spoke. "Duh... duh... dead."

"Skip!" Maggie said, walking towards the door. "Skip? Where's Less?" Her eyes moved to the gun over the man's shoulder. She recognized it as her own.

For a moment, Skip only shook his head. The others started to crowd around. Even Ronnie Eaves staggered out of his booth and began to approach.

"What's going on?" Ronnie asked, rubbing his eyes.

Skip moved to the pool table in the center of the room and sat down the gun and knife. "Less is dead."

A gasp escaped Dizzy Vaughn's lips. "What do you mean, dead?" he coughed.

Again, Skip just shook his head. Anne helped Seth over to the pool table where he leaned on its rail.

Maggie's eyes, wide with fear, darted between them. "Mr. Landon? Skip? What happened?"

Skip turned his back to the table and pushed himself up so that he was sitting on it. "Seth and I found that the front window of the station was broken in. We walked around back and found the back door wide open. Less was in the back hallway." Skip looked up at Maggie and the fear she found in his eyes only intensified her own. Maggie had never seen such a mark of fear on her old friend's face.

Continuing, Skip looked at the floor. "There was blood everywhere... poor Less had to be lying in an inch of it. He had no... he had no..." Skip brought up a hand and wiped his eyes with his thumb and forefinger. "It looked like someone lopped off the top of his head with a scythe."

Nancy Pruitt brought her hand up to cover her mouth. Anne looked at her husband and felt cold. Dizzy Vaughn lit a cigarette.

"See!" Ronnie shouted. "See! I told ya, but nobody would listen! Same as old lady Meadows. Somebody shot him in the fucking head!"

"Nobody shot anybody!" Skip's voice was hard but controlled. He brought his head up and looked at Maggie. "He wasn't shot, Mags. I'm serious when I say that it looked like someone cut off the top of his head… or bit it off."

"Maybe it was an animal attack, then?" Jim chimed in, but Seth started to shake his head in unison with Skip.

"No," Seth said. "It was no animal. Whoever killed Mr. Huggard also destroyed the radio."

Maggie suddenly felt like she was in one of those Hitchcock movies. She felt like she was in one of those scenes where everything has gone all haywire and the camera is staying on her horrified face while everything in the background goes out of focus.

Mrs. Meadows was dead.

Less Huggard was dead.

The phones were dead.

The power was out.

Maggie's fear froze her, and as such she didn't hear the first part of what Jim Pruitt was saying.

"That's it! Nancy, get your coat on. We're getting the hell out of this burg!"

Skip moved off of the table and stood up straight. "Just what do you mean?"

Jim almost laughed. "I mean we're getting the hell out of here. You've got some wacko running around taking scalps, and I don't intend for either me or my wife to be next!"

"Are you kidding me?" Skip took a step after Jim as the man moved towards the bar. "That's a lake-effect blizzard out there, mister. One of the worst I've seen, and I've been living in these parts for going on fifty years. How do you think you're going to get anywhere in this weather?"

Jim pulled his jacket on. Nancy was hesitantly pulling on her gloves. "That's why they call them snowmobiles!" Jim barked.

Nancy put a hand on her husband's shoulder. "Honey, maybe we should…"

"We're leaving, Nancy. That's all there is to it. We'll stick to the road and take the sleds up to Sanborn. Let's go."

What was happening finally dawned on Maggie. "I don't think that's a very good idea, Mr. Pruitt."

Nancy looked at her, her eyes pleading with Maggie to convince Jim to stay in Catchville.

Maggie took a deep breath and gave it a try. "Mr. Pruitt, even with your snowmobile's headlight you're not going to be able to see…"

"How much do I owe you, Ms. Bennington?" Jim interrupted. "For the room, I mean."

There was no give in the man's eyes. Maggie knew then and there that he intended to leave no matter what she or anyone else had to say. "No charge, Mr. Pruitt. Just leave the key on the desk when you go."

"Fine," Jim led his wife to the tavern's door and then stopped. Turning, he said, "It's been nice meeting you all, but… well, we'll go to the police as soon as we get to Sanborn."

No one in the bar replied.

Jim opened up the tavern door and led his wife out into the night. When the door shut behind them Skip walked over and turned the lock.

"I hope they'll be all right," Anne muttered, leaning into Seth.

"Ha!" A burst of smoke escaped Dizzy's lips. "Weather like this? There's apt to be six-foot drifts across the highway. I don't care what kind of sleds they've got, they've got a long hard haul ahead of 'em."

Anne's eyes grew wide. "Why didn't you tell them that?" She looked to Maggie. "Why didn't you tell them that?" she repeated.

Maggie shook her head. "Do you think he would've listened to me, Mrs. Landon?"

The two women traded a long stare before Anne looked away. "No. I suppose not."

February 13th

Catchville, Wisconsin

9:08 p.m. CST

Jim and Nancy were putting their snowmobile suits on in their hotel room. Jim had used his cigarette lighter to light their way into the hotel, and once in the room they lit the kerosene lamp that Maggie had provided.

Nancy was on the verge of tears. "What if we don't make it to Sanborn?" she asked, packing up the few things she'd taken out when they'd arrived.

"What do you mean?"

Now the tears did come. "I mean there's a hell of a lot of snow out there, Jimmy! What happens if one of the sleds turns over? What happens if whoever is out there gets us?"

Jim pulled on his hat and grabbed his helmet off of the dresser. "Don't get hysterical!" His voice was rough, like it got when one of the kids got into trouble. "We'll be on the sleds! No one's going to catch up with us. And as for one of us turning over... it's not going to happen. We're not going to follow the trail. We're going to stay on the highway all the way up to Sanborn. We'll be fine... because we'll be out of here."

Nancy opened her mouth to protest and then shut it back up. Some part of her, some hidden part deep in the recesses of her mind was shivering. It was intuition, but it was more than that. Some part of her that Nancy didn't want to admit was there was screaming that they shouldn't leave Catchville. But she'd say nothing more. Jim's mind was made up, and she'd follow him to the ends of the earth.

February 13th

Catchville, Wisconsin

9:16 p.m. CST

Outside the Bennington, Jim cleared the snow off of his snowmobile's seat. Why did Nancy have to get so rattled? Couldn't she see that they were doing the right thing? To stay here in Catchville was insane. He was about to mount up when he saw that his wife was having a hard time packing her bag in the rear compartment of her sled. With a grunt he moved over, gently nudged her out of the way and did it himself. He slammed the top of the compartment door and looked at her.

"You ready?" he shouted. It was hard enough to hear what they were saying through their helmets on a cloudless day, but with this wind, it was damn near impossible. She did, however, and nodded her head. Jim shortly wondered if she was still crying under that visor and then put the thought out of his mind. In a few hours they'd be in a warm bed in Sanborn and then she'd be thanking him in more ways than one.

They started up their snowmobiles and clicked on their headlights. Jim was dismayed to see just how little the lights helped. For the entire ride they weren't going to be able to see more than a dozen feet in front of their faces. Oh well, he thought, as long as we stick to the road we'll be fine. Who else was going to be out on a night like this?

Jim took the lead, steering to the center of the road and heading east. At least the wind will be at our backs, he thought. He glanced back to make sure Nancy was behind him and then gunned his throttle a bit. He certainly wasn't going to go full bore in this mess, but he would breathe easier once they were out of Catchville.

To his right, Jim looked towards Maggie's Tavern. The

snow was furious enough now that he couldn't see the building from the road. He turned his head back forward and found that his snowmobile had drifted a bit to the right while he had his head turned. *Hey now,* he told himself, *keep your eyes on the road, buddy.* A thought then occurred to Jim that he hadn't thought of before. From the rough directions he'd heard in Maggie's Tavern, they'd soon be passing the house where the old lady—Mrs. Meadows was her name—was lying dead on her living room floor, shot or otherwise.

Jim shivered as the sled whined forward. He kept glancing to the side of the road, not wanting to see where the old woman's house was, and yet wanting to see it at the same time. Until he knew they were past it he was going to keep looking for it. He didn't have to wait long. Soon they passed a snow-covered drive. The tiny house was close enough to the road that Jim got a quick glance at it before it was gone. As soon as it was past, Jim let out a sigh of relief and smiled beneath his helmet. He was so relieved, in fact, that he turned to give his wife a thumbs-up.

Jim almost lost control of his sled. *Nancy wasn't behind him!*

His smile vanished in an instant. *Jesus!* he thought. *Can't she keep up?* Pulling his thumb off of the throttle, Jim angled his sled to the far left of the road. He stopped there and waited for a few seconds. *Come on, Nancy. Where are you?* After a full minute, he turned his sled back to the right and arced across the road to turn around.

Jim followed his own track west. Where could she be? He hoped against hope that she hadn't taken her eyes off of the road for a few seconds and gone into the ditch. In this wind he wouldn't have heard it.

It only took him twenty seconds or so of backtracking before he saw her sled at the side of the road.

Nancy's snowmobile was on its side.

"God all mighty!" Jim yelled beneath his visor. He veered his snowmobile to the right side of the road and stopped. His helmet was off in seconds. Jim ran over to where Nancy's sled was and the horror of what he saw in the snow made his breath hitch. He followed her sled's track to the center of the road with his eyes and then with his feet.

There was a set of footprints running out from the other side of the highway. Jim could see where someone ran out and pushed Nancy off of her snowmobile! He could see the mark where she'd landed in the road, and there...

Jim let loose a long moan. The footprints moved over to where Nancy had landed and then... drag marks into the woods.

"Nancy!" Jim cried, though it came out sounding muted in the hard wind. "No!" He sprinted in pursuit of the drag marks. The snow in the ditch was deeper than that on the road and Jim fell face first into the snow. It took him only moments to get up in his panic and terror; he didn't even feel the icy wetness that now coated his face.

At the edge of the thick bramble he halted. Jim scanned the woods with his eyes but the damn snow was just too thick! His gaze couldn't penetrate the trees more than a few feet in front of his face.

"The track..." he muttered. The blizzard was preventing him from seeing what was in front of him, but it did provide a temporary track to follow. Jim poured into the bramble, pushing aside the clawing branches with his hands. His face was scraped more than once, but he didn't feel that either.

The drag mark curved off to the left and Jim followed it. The density of the bramble he clawed through was thicker here, but it didn't matter. The only thing that did matter was finding Nancy. Even as he struggled, the first vestiges of guilt were starting to penetrate his mind. *"What if we don't make it to Sanborn?"* His wife's words hit his memory like a sledgehammer.

"Nancy!" Jim cried out again, knowing it was useless. "Nancy?"

All at once he broke through the edge of the bramble. Surrounding him now were low sweeping pine branches doused in snow. The going became easier and Jim moved faster. Within the stretches of the pine trees, the wind was blocked and he could hear the sound of his own labored breathing. He was racing in sheer panic now. The almost pitch blackness made it difficult to see on the snow but Jim felt like he had no time to pause.

He tripped.

Though the snow was deep, Jim hit the ground hard. He glanced at his feet to see what he'd tripped over.

It was her.

"Nancy! Nancy!" Jim scrambled around on his knees. Her helmet was off. Her eyes were open... but there was no life in them. Jim leaned close to her head. "Nancy? What's wrong?"

Inches from her face, Jim could now see the blood. A thick line of it ran down over her temple to her cheek and chin. "Oh, God!"

Something struck Jim hard in the center of his back. On instinct, he turned and swung wildly with his right fist. He connected, but what he hit felt unmovable, like a block of granite. Something clenched his shoulder with enough strength to break bone. Jim recoiled, ducking his chin into his chest. When he did, he caught sight of a white hand squeezing through his jacket and sweater, and into his flesh.

Jim screamed.

When he first looked up, all he saw was a black hole of a mouth moving towards his head. Now on his back, Jim shot his left hand up to prevent the mouth from reaching him. His hand connected with his attacker's face and for the moment, halted the onslaught. A brief lull in the wind was all it took for Jim to get a hearty mouthful of a foul, wet odor that made his intestines constrict.

In the midst of the retch Jim heard a snarl. His arm was

batted away and he was pinned to the ground. Jim gasped at the barest glimpse he caught of a pair of foggy blue eyes and then...

The pain at the top of his head was brief, at least.

February 13th, 2007

Catchville, Wisconsin

9:04 p.m. CST

It was only a short time after Jim and Nancy left that Dizzy Vaughn started talking about guns.

"Hell if I'm going to be without my rifle if there's some nut-job running around town!"

Maggie was doing her best to talk him out of it. "Look, Dizzy. Who knows who's out there in the dark? Do you really think it's worth the risk to walk over to your house to get a gun? That nut-job you're talking about might be waiting for you in your bedroom when you get there!"

The old man shook his head. "Nobody better be in my house without my permission or they're liable to get strung up from the ceiling…"

"Shut up, Dizz'." Skip's words weren't loud but they had the desired effect. "We don't need any more than one gun right now. We'll end up shooting each other. Maggie, you got more shells for this, right?" Skip pointed to the shotgun on the pool table.

The bartender nodded. "There's two boxes full in the storeroom."

"All right." Skip took a deep breath and seemed to mull over their situation.

Anne had helped Seth back to one of the booths and they now sat looking at each other.

"Are you going to be all right, Seth?" Her husband still had that blank, stony look in his eyes. "Seth?"

Slowly, he shook his head. The lower lids of his eyes started to shine as they filled with tears. "Anne..." he started, his lips parting only slightly. "Anne..."

She grasped his hands with her own. They felt cold, like stone, and all at once Anne became more worried about her husband than anything that might be out in the dark waiting for them. "Seth," she whispered, "honey, it's okay."

"It was awful, Anne. It was awful. His head was just... just... gone."

"I know sweetie," she answered, knowing full well that she had no idea of the horror Seth had witnessed. When Anne was in college she tried her hand at writing a few horror stories, but she found it much more difficult than the historical fiction she normally wrote. Writing horror took something she just didn't possess. Anne had the imagination, she could visualize terrible things in her mind, but they just never seemed *real* to her the way details did in other stories she wrote. She found that she just didn't want to think about awful things that went bump in the night. She found that she just didn't want to think about how people reacted to things that scared them, and in the process she found that she couldn't really scare anyone with her prose if she didn't want to think about anyone being scared in the first place. And as far as real life went, Anne had never experienced anything really, truly terrifying outside of a Hollywood thriller—knock on wood. She'd never seen a dead person outside of a casket in a funeral home, and Anne didn't think that funeral home corpses were really that scary.

No. Anne just didn't have anything personal to draw on that could really tell her just how terrified Seth was, but she wouldn't tell him that.

"It's okay. Go ahead and tell me about it... or don't tell me about it. It's all right."

To her surprise, Seth let loose a short laugh and said, "I don't think I'm ever going to be able to lie in bed before going to sleep and not see that man's bloody head in my mind."

Anne squeezed his hands. "Yes you will, Seth. This *will* pass. This *will* go away." She didn't know if it would or not, but if Seth didn't believe that there was a glimmer of hope of forgetting this terrible night, he was going to lose it. "It just seems like it'll be there forever right now, babe. But it will go away. I promise."

His eyes softened a bit as he listened to her. He bit his lip and nodded, "Yeah. You're right. It just seems so…"

Before he could finish, a yell from the bar broke into their conversation.

"Well fuck that!" Ronnie Eaves' hair was standing out at all angles from the evening's ordeals. "I'm not going anywhere! I'm not getting my damn head shot off! I'm staying right here, damn it!"

Maggie walked right up to Ronnie and started talking to him in a low voice. Anne and Seth looked at each other.

"I suppose we better go find out what this is all about," Seth said, "the last person I want making decisions is him."

Anne nodded and stood. She couldn't believe how relieved she was to hear her husband speaking in such a rational matter. Anne knew she'd have to watch him, though. Seth was fragile. Sure, he put on a decent front of being a man's man and all that, but he was no Indiana Jones. He was good at masking his feelings, but Anne knew that what he'd seen in that gas station would stick with him for some time to come.

"What's this all about?" Seth whispered to Skip who was standing near the pool table.

The older man held up a finger, "Just a minute."

Ronnie shook his head violently in response to whatever Maggie was saying to him.

"What the hell, Eaves," Dizzy said from near the jukebox, "you stay here and you're going to end up an Eskimo pie. You won't need no nut-job to shoot ya up, you'll just freeze to death."

"Go to hell, Dizzy!" Ronnie spat.

"That's enough!" Maggie looked back and forth between the two men. "The heat's down here in the bar. We all know that the power probably won't come back on until tomorrow morning. In the meantime, it's going to get cold in here, maybe not freeze-to-death cold, but cold enough to get very, very uncomfortable. The first floor of the hotel has heat. The generator will have kicked in by now. If we all move over there together, if Skip mans the shotgun, we'll be fine. Once we get in the hotel we'll just lock up the place and hold out until morning."

Ronnie threw his arms up. "Oh! Well! We know from what Skip and that other fella said that the killer don't have no qualms about breaking windows, so we should be just fine in the hotel!"

Maggie had just about had it with the young man, "Ronnie," her voice sharpened at his name, "if you want to stay here, then stay here. *Alone.*"

The implications of spending the night alone in the bar slowly worked into the man's mind. He began to shake his head. "I don't believe this. I don't believe you're just going to make a stupid-ass decision and force me to come along."

Maggie turned away from him and walked to the end of the bar.

"You bitch," Ronnie said this silently, but in the quiet bar it was still very clear. Skip moved at once with a speed and surety that Anne couldn't believe he possessed. Before Ronnie knew what was happening, Skip grabbed the hair at the back of the younger man's head and pushed him into the bar. He held Ronnie there, pushing his cheek down on the rail.

"Hey! Hey…" Ronnie's words became garbled as his face was pushed down harder on the bar.

Skip leaned down close to the man's head and began to speak. "I don't care if you're drunk or not, Ronnie, that's no way to speak to a lady, especially Ms. Bennington. Do you hear me?"

The younger man's pleas came out as hostile gibberish. "Hmmrgh! Hmmrgh!"

Skip pushed Ronnie's head down harder, silencing him, "I think you'd better apologize for acting like an ass. What do you say?" He pushed down hard enough to produce grunts of pain from Ronnie's clenched lips before letting up completely.

"Apologize to her."

Ronnie brought his head up and for a moment everyone in the bar thought he was going to go right at Skip. Mrs. Meadows and Less Huggard were dead, and now Ronnie Eaves was going to start a fight in the darkened tavern. Perhaps the insanity of this wasn't lost on the young man. After a moment of giving Skip the meanest glare he could manage, he looked across the bar and then at the floor.

"Sorry Maggie," he muttered.

Maggie replied at once. "It's all right, Ronnie. I know what kind of pressure we're all under, but we've got to keep our heads. The fact is, we can't stay here. It's going to get too cold. We need to go."

This time, no one protested.

February 13th, 2007

Catchville, Wisconsin

9:36 p.m. CST

It took some doing to get prepared for the walk across the street. For starters, the tavern had to be prepared for a night without power. The water faucets were all turned on to a pencil-thin stream to avoid any cracked pipes. With Ronnie and Skip's help, all the beer cases and kegs were dragged into the storage room and covered with blankets. Audrey went around the tavern with a flashlight and pulled the plug on everything with a cord so that when the power came back on the fuses wouldn't crash. Skip loaded the shotgun, shoved as many shells as he could into his jacket pockets, and put the rest in a paper sack. Finally, all seven of them were standing around the front door of Maggie's tavern, zipping up their coats and pulling on their gloves and hats.

"I've been thinking," Dizzy spoke up, "when we get over there, where we gonna stay? I don't think it'll be at all smart to split up into the rooms. If there is someone out there gunning for us we'll just be making it a hell of a lot easier by splittin' up."

Maggie and Skip exchanged a long look.

"He's right," Ronnie said with satisfaction. "See, we shouldn't go anywhere. We should stay put."

Maggie shook her head, "No. We'll all stay in my apartment. It might be a bit cramped, but choosing between cramped and dead, I'll take cramped."

Opening up the shotgun, Skip double-checked to make sure it was loaded, "All right. Dizzy's gonna move the slowest so we'll put him in front. Ronnie, you walk alongside of him. Maggie and Audrey behind them, Seth and Anne behind them. I'll bring up the rear with the gun. Everybody stick close to each other. This blizzard's a bad one, and you can't see more than ten feet in front of yourself, so stick together."

"Everybody ready?" Maggie asked.

Ronnie rubbed his temples, "Shit, no."

"Good," Skip stepped to the door and looked out the diamond-shaped window. "Let's go."

The door was thrown open. Skip stepped aside and waved out Ronnie and Dizzy, then Maggie and her niece, and finally Seth and Anne.

Anne was amazed at the ferocity of the storm. The wind caught them like sails as soon as they left the relative shelter of the doorway. Squinting, she held tight onto Seth's hand and kept her eyes on Maggie's back. Seth's flashlight was doing little to help light their way and it made Anne wonder just how Seth and Skip had managed to get all the way over to the gas station. In the midst of the blizzard, Anne found that her fear of being ambushed by some deranged maniac had vanished. How could anyone attack them in weather like this? That is, unless said maniac was waiting for them at the hotel.

As they were all following Dizzy Vaughn, they moved slowly—but as deep as the snow was, Anne didn't think they could have moved much faster if they'd wanted to. Just as she was wondering how much further they had to go, Anne looked ahead and saw Dizzy and Ronnie rise into the air as they climbed the Bennington's front steps.

Safe, Anne thought.

Maggie moved between the two men and unlocked the door with her keys. In seconds, all seven of them filed inside with Skip bringing up the rear. He slammed the door and turned the lock.

Though the lobby was warm, it was very dark with only the three flashlights providing light. Instinctively, all seven of them stomped the snow from their boots.

"I've got lanterns in the apartment," Maggie said. She started to lead the way around the hotel's front desk.

Anne turned to see how Seth was doing, and when she did she caught a glimpse of something moving out on the porch. She was transfixed for a moment, staring at the figure that wasn't much more than a shadow outside the window. Anne was questioning whether she was really seeing something or not when the figure moved to the side and out of view. Seth caught the stunned look in his wife's eye.

"What is it?" he whispered.

Anne spoke, stuttering, "Some… someone's out on the porch."

They all looked. Three flashlight beams lit up the frosted front windows of the hotel.

"I don't see anything," Ronnie whispered.

"It was there," Anne pointed, "I saw it there. It moved out of sight."

There were a few more seconds of ominous silence as Maggie, Ronnie and Seth scanned the windows with their lights.

Without taking his eyes off of the windows, Seth whispered, "Are you sure, babe?"

Anne whispered as well, "Yes. It was there, in that window. It--"

The sound of breaking glass came from their left. The seven of them jumped and the three flashlight beams were shined down the hallway that led to the first floor hotel rooms.

"Oh my God! Oh my God!" Ronnie hissed. "Shit! It's in! It's in!"

They all listened for any further sign of the intruder. Anne watched the hall with wide eyes expecting to see one of the hotel room doors open at any moment, but after close to a minute of anxious waiting, they heard and saw nothing.

As usual, Maggie was first to react logically, "Let's all quietly move into the apartment," she whispered. "Come on."

One by one the seven of them filed around the desk and through the doorway. Skip brought up the rear, walking backwards and leveling the gun at the hallway all the while.

Anne followed Audrey through the doorway and saw that it was an antechamber of sorts. No larger than a walk-in closet, one wall of the room held a few dozen open-ended mailbox slots and the other a wooden desk piled with papers.

Maggie led the way through the door on the other end of the small room, and once they were all through she shut the door, turned the deadbolt and put up the chain.

February 13th, 2007

Catchville, Wisconsin

9:48 p.m. CST

Once inside the door to Maggie's apartment, they found themselves inside a short hall. To the left was a doorway to a tiny kitchen. To the right was the dining room.

With the shotgun still in his hands, Skip leaned against the closed door, "Get some light, Mags."

Maggie moved into the kitchen, lit a kerosene lantern, and then lit another in the dining room.

"Now what?" Ronnie whispered.

Skip turned and inspected the lock on the door. After a moment he turned back to the rest of them, "Let's go back and have a seat. I think this lock will hold if anybody tries to get in."

"Is there another door?" Seth asked.

Maggie shook her head, "Nope. That's the only way in or out." She led the way down the short hall. Two doors lay off of it on the left, one was a bedroom and the other a bathroom, and another bedroom lay off of the hall on the right. At the end of the hall was a small living room holding a couch, a rocking chair, a recliner and a television set.

"I'll get some more chairs," Maggie opened up a closet on one end of the living room and pulled two metal folding chairs. She then used a match to light yet another kerosene lamp on the coffee table.

"You must get those things wholesale," Seth quipped, though there was no humor in his voice.

"Like I said when you folks came in, we get quite a few of

these lake effect storms in the winter, and the power is prone to going out. You live here long enough and you learn to be prepared."

Everyone sat down except for Skip who kept looking back down the hall.

Ronnie was the first to speak up, his voice cracking as he did, "Like I said, what's next?"

"The windows," Audrey said. "Shouldn't we cover them up or something?" There were two windows in the living room, one on the north wall and one on the west. Both were currently framed by thick drapes.

Dizzy shook his head, reached inside his jacket and pulled his cigarettes from his shirt pocket, "They got locks on 'em. It seems to me that if anybody tries to get in through those windows, Skip'll have their head blown off in two shakes."

Maggie agreed, "We don't have anything to cover them up with anyhow, unless we want to start moving the dressers around…"

"So we just sit here?" Ronnie said.

Anne, who'd been sitting next to Ronnie, found that she'd had quite enough of the man's coffee-flavored beer breath. She stood up, went over to the window, and cupped her hand against the glass to peek outside. The darkened windows provided little in the way of a view. Anne guessed that unless something was pressed right up against them, there wouldn't be able to see much.

Ronnie was still protesting, "Are we just gonna sit here until the cops come? Are we just gonna wait until whoever is out there comes for us? Until we end up like Old Lady Meadows? Or Less?"

"I don't get you, Eaves," Dizzy said, puffing on his smoke. "First you don't want to leave the tavern, now you don't want to stay here. Make up your damn mind."

"I've had just about all I'm gonna take from you, Dizz'. If you don't…"

"Quiet!" Skip said through gritted teeth. His eyes were locked on the hallway. "I think I hear something,"

They all watched Skip creep down the hall towards the apartment's front door. Seth stood and followed him. A dull, irregular thumping sound could be heard from the lobby. Skip stopped and cast an eye back towards Seth—they were both thinking the same thought.

Whoever was on the other side of that door was the one who cut off the top of Less Huggard's head.

There was another bang from the lobby followed by several high-pitched clangs. It sounded like someone had knocked the old-fashioned cash register off of the counter and onto the floor. Seth and Skip stood looking at each other, listening. For ten seconds, twenty, thirty, neither heard anything. Finally, Skip gripped the shotgun with both hands and slowly moved towards the door. Seth followed, but this time he widened the distance between them to a good six feet. If something came through that door all of a sudden, Seth wanted to have a few seconds to figure out what to do.

Skip moved past the kitchen and dining room and was now close enough to touch the door with the barrel of the gun. He stopped, and Seth did the same.

Cocking his head slightly, Skip's eyes centered on the doorknob and in his mind he imagined that soon it would start to turn. The door was locked, but whoever was out in the lobby knocking things around wouldn't necessarily know that. In his mind's eye he saw that knob turn as the predator tested the door. Skip made a decision; as soon as he saw the knob turn, he was going to fire a double round into the door. The shot might not penetrate it—indeed it probably wouldn't—but it would let whoever was on the other side of that door know that he wasn't fooling around.

Skip stood motionless and waited another thirty seconds. The knob didn't move. The sounds from the lobby had stopped, and Skip found that he was scared to death. When Seth tapped him on the shoulder, he jumped.

"Sorry," Seth whispered. "There's a keyhole." Seth pointed at the door and Skip saw that, sure enough, the lock on the door had an old-fashioned keyhole. "You can look through it," Seth continued.

A slight grin turned up at the corner of Skip's mouth. "I can look, huh?"

Seth grinned back and whispered, "You want me to look?"

Skip shook his head. "I don't want anybody between me and that door." He lifted the gun up to emphasize the point.

Visibly relieved, Seth nodded.

Skip stepped right up to the door. The light provided by the lamps in the kitchen and dining room of the apartment were sufficient to illuminate the hall, but Seth knew that there were no lights on in the lobby. Turning, he motioned for Seth's flashlight. He carefully took it in one hand while holding the shotgun in the other. He waited yet another few moments, listening, before leaning down to the keyhole. Skip took a deep breath, thumbed on the light, positioned it towards the lock, and looked.

Skip expected to see one of two things. He expected to see either the expanse of the tiny mailroom and the backside of the lobby desk beyond, or he expected to see the legs or hand of whoever had killed Mrs. Meadows and Less.

He saw neither.

What Skip was seeing took a moment to process. Out of all the things he'd expected to see, a flat, colored disc was none of them. Skip tilted his head in an attempt to discern what the hell he was looking at. Taking up the entire keyhole was... well, *blueness*. There was something colored a solid, icy blue on the other side of the door.

As Skip watched, confused, the blueness *blinked.*

"Ah!" Skip yelled and fumbled backwards onto his butt. A slew of murmurs erupted from down the hall.

"What is it?" Seth whispered as he reached to help Skip up. "What is it?"

Skip shook his head. He was about to speak when a massive *THUD* echoed forth from the door. The first was followed by several more that came in quick succession. A scream that Skip thought he recognized as being from Audrey erupted from the living room. Ronnie Eaves cursed in the form of a shout, and still the pounding continued. As Skip struggled to get to his feet his eyes never left the door. He could see the wood shake with every *THUD*. He could see just how far the edge at the top of the door was moving inside the doorjamb with each hit. The door wasn't going to hold. Whoever was out there had incredible strength.

As if reading his thoughts, Skip heard Seth's wife yelling from behind them, "It's gonna come through!"

Another hit registered on the door caused the center of it to crack with a sound like breaking ice. The sight of that crack urged Skip into action. Getting to one knee, he waved off Seth, pointed the shotgun at the door and pulled the trigger. The shot sounded like a thunderclap in such close quarters.

The pounding stopped.

Skip brought his head up from the gun to inspect the damage. The majority of the door was still in tact, though there were splintered, pin-sized holes from the shot spray that penetrated all the way through. For the moment no one moved. No one spoke.

A faint, low growl emanated from behind the door. Skip and Seth looked at each other, eyes wide, as the growl continued. Terrified, Skip fumbled his hand into the pocket of his coat, pulled out two more shells, and reloaded. When he slapped the shotgun closed, the growling on the other side of the door stopped.

Seth raised an eyebrow. Skip shrugged. For a dozen long moments, the only sound in the short hallway was the breathing of the two men.

Maggie stepped up behind them. She tapped first Seth, then Skip on their shoulders, pointed at the door and made a questioning expression with her eyes.

Skip stood up straight and gave Seth and Maggie a silent command to stay back. They nodded their assent.

As the lobby was dark, Skip could see nothing but blackness through those tiny holes the shot-spray had created in the door. Skip knew he'd have to get right up to the door and shine the flashlight through the keyhole once more. He just didn't know what he'd do, though, if he saw that blinking, blue eye once more. What the hell was on the other side of the door? He and Seth had deduced that it was a man that had killed Less since whoever had done it had also destroyed the radio. Why would an animal destroy the radio? That was all fine and well, but the growl they'd just heard didn't sound like a man.

"Shit," Skip exhaled. Holding the gun tightly in his hands, he stepped close enough to the door to smell the newly exposed wood. He squinted, trying to see if he couldn't see something through the tiny holes in the door. For the life of him he didn't want to have to look through that keyhole again. If he could just—

Skip had no time to react, not even time to scream, as a white fist punched through the door in line with his head and grabbed his throat.

He heard the gun fire another double round, but he knew it wasn't pointed at the door. It was pointed at the floor. The grip that the hand had on his neck was like an iron band. No air was permitted in or out of his lungs. Before Skip knew what was happening, the white hand pulled Skip's head into the door. He saw several, tiny glinting specks of light in his field of vision and had a half second's worth of consciousness to think, *that's what they mean by 'seeing stars'*, before everything went black.

January 29th, 2007

Cable, Wisconsin

12:01 p.m. CST

Earl Meisner pulled the clock-shaped sign off the counter and wound the hands so that it read, BE BACK AT 12:30. He paused, thinking that it had been a while since he and Patty had had a nooner, and repositioned the hands to 12:45. Earl hung the sign on the inside of the shop door with a smile and pulled his keys from his pocket.

He pulled on his sunglasses and was about to head outside when he saw a blue sedan come tearing into the lot. The car fishtailed and the rear bumper barely missed the pole supporting Earl's brand new sign that read MEISNER POLARIS in bright green letters.

"What the…?" Earl pushed open the door and started outside. Whoever this dipshit was, he was going to get an earful for pulling into the lot like that! Earl pressed his chew into his lip with his tongue before spitting a brown stream into the snow.

The driver of the car—a bearded guy with cool eyes—slid the car into park a dozen feet from the front of the shop. Yup, this moron was gonna get an earful.

"You work here?" the man asked as he hurried out of the car.

Earl put his hands in the pockets of his jacket. "I'm the owner, and you got a helluva lotta nerve pulling in here like that."

The driver of the sedan didn't seem to be listening as he stepped to the back seat of the car and opened it up. "I need a sled." He pulled an immense black duffle bag from the backseat. "And I need it quick." The stranger reached back into the car and pulled out another bag.

Earl had been about ready to give the stranger another piece of advice—something to the effect that if the man wanted to stay conscious he'd better think twice about pulling into Meisner Polaris like that again—but when Earl saw that second bag, he closed his mouth. Earl had done enough hunting in his life to know a gun bag when he saw one.

The stranger slammed the back door of the car shut with his foot and started towards the shop. "I said I need a sled and I need one now!"

The severity of the man's tone got Earl's attention, "Uh, sure. I guess. Come on in."

The stranger dropped both his bags as soon as he was inside the door and then glanced around at all the snowmobiles on the showroom floor, "That one," he said, pointing to a brand new Polaris Black Widow.

Earl was beginning to get suspicious, "Why do you need a sled so quick, if you don't mind me asking…"

"I do mind," The stranger removed his wallet from his pocket and opened it up. He removed a folded piece of paper and handed it to Earl. "That's the title to my car. I'll trade you the car and say… five-hundred for the sled."

Earl started to unravel the paper and then looked over the stranger's shoulder to the lot outside, "That's a brand new car."

"I know it is."

Smiling, Earl shook his head, "Look, mister, this is all a might strange. It's not everyday that I get somebody coming in with a gun telling me they'll trade a brand new car for a snowmobile."

The stranger waved his hand, "Then this is your lucky day." He pulled his driver's license from his wallet and handed it over. "Look, I don't have time to explain. I've got twenty minutes to spare at best. I'll give you my car, plus five hundred cash, for the sled. You're making a profit of about five grand, plus whatever you marked the sled up from. Get on the horn, call the police or whoever, and give them my name. When you find out I'm not a fugitive or haven't stolen anything or whatever you might think I might be up to, I want you to gas up that sled."

"Well…" Earl didn't have the slightest idea of what to say.

The stranger picked up his bags and walked them to the shop's counter. He set them down at its side, "Watch my bags, and if you look inside them, I'll know. I'm going to the restaurant across the highway to get something to eat. Have that sled ready when I get back!"

The stranger walked over and left the shop, the bells above the door jingling.

Earl looked down at the driver's license. *Helman Graff.* Now there's a strange name, he thought. Leaning over, Earl spit in the trashcan and looked at his watch. Twenty minutes. He supposed he'd better make a call to the police department and find out what this guy's story was.

February 13th, 2007

Catchville, Wisconsin

10:00 p.m. CST

Seth's reaction was instinctive. If he'd had time to think, he might not have acted, so it was probably best that he didn't. He jumped forward and grabbed the arm that had busted through the door. Skip, his eyes closed, was still being held by the throat as who—or what—ever was on the other side of the door tried to pull him through.

The first thing that Seth felt when he got hold of the arm was how cold it was. The attacker was wearing some kind of thin, gabardine jacket, but its thinness didn't explain why the arm felt so cold. The second thing Seth felt was the sheer strength of the attacker. Though he had a good grip on the arm and was twisting and pushing, Seth felt like he had hold of the trunk of a tree. The arm was unmovable.

"Help!" Seth yelled, and saw Maggie heading towards him. He thought she meant to grab the gun from the floor, but she didn't. She dodged to the right and went into the kitchen.

"Help me!" Seth yelled again. The attacker was pulling Skip into the door and Seth thought that at any moment the man's head would crack through the wood. The strength of that arm was unreal.

Ronnie ran up, his eyes wide with fear, and grabbed onto the attacker's hand. He attempted to pull back the white fingers that had Skip in a stranglehold, but it was no use. The attacker's hand was attached to Skip's neck like a vice.

"Look out!" Maggie yelled. Seth glanced back over his shoulder and saw her coming. He let go of the arm as Skip's head was slammed into the door once more. The wood creaked and splintered under the impact. In the lamplight, Seth saw a glint of steel. A second later Maggie brought down the butcher knife on the attacker's arm.

In that first hack, the blade of the knife sunk an eighth of an inch into the attacker's white skin. However, there was no jerk or retreat of the attack. In fact, the fingers about Skip's neck only seemed to flex and tighten. Blood oozed out of the wound and in the low light it looked black.

Ronnie let go of the clenched fingers when Maggie brought the knife down, and though he moaned at the sight of the blood, he shouted out frantic encouragement, "Hit him again Mags! Hit him again!"

With gritted teeth, Maggie Bennington brought down the knife once more with both hands. The blade sunk into the arm with a flat sound, and a spray of black blood misted up into Maggie's face. A cross between a howl and a scream erupted from behind the door. The fingers around Skip's neck straightened and Skip fell to the floor in a heap. Maggie pulled on the knife and dislodged it from the arm with some effort. The hand thrashed out, its fingers stretching and clawing for anyone within reach.

"Look out!" Maggie yelled. Ronnie stepped back from the door as the white fingers missed his face by inches.

Maggie took the knife in her right hand and began to slash repeatedly at the hand. On the second slash the blade cut the palm, and with another she caught the tips of the knuckles.

The arm retreated through the door.

Seth worked on instinct now, yelling, "Grab the flashlight!"

Ronnie only looked at the hole in the door while Seth shoved past and picked up the shotgun from the floor. The gun felt heavy in his hands. Seth had never shot a gun in his life, but he figured it couldn't be that hard—just point the damn thing and pull the trigger, right?

"Ronnie!" Seth yelled, realizing that the man hadn't moved.

"Pick up the flashlight!"

The young man snapped out of his trance. Picking up the light, he thumbed it on and pointed it at the door.

Skip let out a low moan on the floor and rolled to the side. Maggie crouched to help him as Seth and Ronnie stared at the hole in the door. Another low howl came from somewhere out in the lobby. Seth gauged that it was safe to get right up to the door and he motioned for Ronnie to do the same.

The beam of light illuminated the small antechamber outside the door. Ronnie adjusted the level of the beam and a section of the lobby became visible. Both Ronnie and Seth gasped as they saw the man standing on the far side of the hotel desk holding his arm.

Tall, wearing jeans and a thin black jacket akin to a suit coat, the man had his back to them. His hair—stark white—was long enough to cover the collar of his jacket.

"Shoot him!" Ronnie hissed.

Seth put the end of the barrel through the door. The stranger was in his sights, but Seth didn't pull the trigger. No matter what the guy had done to Skip, no matter what the guy might've done to Less Huggard and Old Lady Meadows, Seth just couldn't justify shooting the stranger in cold blood.

Instead, Seth called out, his voice cracking as he did, "Stay right where you are or I'll shoot!"

The stranger's head turned in a flash and all at once the beam of the flashlight caught his eyes. Both Seth and Ronnie's breath caught as the beam shined on those foggy blue eyes. For a moment, those eyes looked like floating, fluorescent blue disks hanging in front of a white face, then there was a snarl as the stranger bit down on his teeth with an audible *snap*. Quickly—too quickly—the stranger ran out of the two men's line of sight.

Ronnie backed slowly away from the door until he was flush up against the wall. "What..." he stammered, "what on God's green motherfucking earth was that?"

Seth moved away from the door as well, dumbfounded.

February 13th, 2007

Catchville, Wisconsin

10:09 p.m. CST

Audrey, Dizzy and Anne came up the hall. At Maggie's command, Audrey retrieved two pillows from the bedroom and they put them underneath Skip's head on the floor. Audrey suggested that they put him in one of the bedrooms or on the couch but Anne protested, saying that they should make sure that nothing was broken before they tried to move him. Skip's eyes were open but he hadn't said much. Every time he tried, his throat felt like someone was rubbing the inside of it with sandpaper. Anne retrieved a cold washcloth from the kitchen sink and handed it to Maggie. She gently wiped the cloth on Skip's neck, seeing the thick purple bruises there darken as she did.

"Who was it?" Dizzy asked, looking at Seth and Ronnie. "Who the hell was it?"

Seth shook his head. He was still, for the moment at least, speechless.

"Nobody from around here," Ronnie said. "I'd have remembered somebody runnin' around with white hair and white skin like that."

"White hair? White skin?" Dizzy repeated with a raised eyebrow.

Seth nodded as Anne went to him and grabbed onto his hand, "Are you all right?" she asked.

"Yeah," He then looked back to Dizzy. "He was an albino I think…"

Ronnie shook his head, "But 'bino's got pink eyes and that some-bitch didn't have no pink eyes! That guy had…" Eaves didn't know how to continue. He held his hands up to the sides of his head. "That guy had animal eyes!"

A light cough caused spittle to settle at the corner of Skip's mouth, "Git…" his voice sounded like he was speaking into a tin can. "Git…"

"Now, now," Maggie said, moving the washcloth up to Skip's forehead. "Don't try to talk."

Skip gritted his teeth. Something in his mind told him that they were all in very grave danger. The others in Maggie's apartment were acting like there was just a madman on the loose in Catchville, but Skip thought that that was only part of it. Skip had felt the strength of the thing that had grabbed his throat. Skip had felt the cold of the thing that had grabbed his throat. That cold strength was enough to put his mind to work, but with Ronnie and Seth's description of the man, well, Skip thought that they'd better start to wise up.

He swallowed hard and the pain caused small tears to form at the corners of his eyes, "Get… dresser… in front… of door." The words came out in a soft staccato. Maggie only looked at him for a moment before realization crossed her eyes.

Maggie had known Skip Hanson for the better part of twenty-five years. In the last decade and a half there had been plenty of opportunities for the two of them to be alone late into the night at the tavern. There had even been a few times when they'd come close to being more than just friends. Maggie knew Skip better than she knew anyone else, and right now she could see the urgency in his eyes.

She looked up at Ronnie, Seth and Anne, "You three! Get into the bedroom, right now! Move the dresser out in front of the door!"

The three of them only looked at her for a moment.

"Now!" Maggie yelled. She had a sneaking suspicion that whatever had pushed its fist right through the door wouldn't be held back by the dresser for long, but at least it was a start.

While the others went to wrangle the dresser out of the room, Maggie turned her attention back to Skip.

"Is his neck broken, Aunt Maggie?" Audrey asked. The girl was standing in the entranceway to the kitchen hugging herself with her arms.

"I'm not sure. Is your neck broken, Skip?"

In response the man carefully lifted his head up off of the pillows and turned it slowly from side to side.

"I don't think so," Maggie said to herself as much as to her niece. "Let's try and get him into my room, Audrey. Do you think you can stand, Skip?"

While Maggie held onto one of his arms, her niece grabbed the other. Soon they had him into a sitting position. They were about to raise him up off the ground when Skip looked at Maggie, his eyes wide.

"What is it?" she asked. Maggie looked to Audrey, who was also looking at her with a generous portion of unmasked terror. "What?" she repeated.

Skip went to speak but stopped himself. It just hurt too much.

"Aunt Maggie," Audrey said, "the blood on your forehead, from that... *thing*..."

Maggie's hand went to her forehead on instinct. "What?"

"It's *black*, Aunt Maggie! The blood is black!"

Using her finger, Maggie rubbed her forehead and brought it down to look, but the blood had already dried and her finger was clean. "No, it's just dried. It just looks black," she said.

"Na... no," Skip managed. He lifted his arm and pointed to the knife lying on the floor.

Maggie turned and picked up the knife. She held it up and looked at the blade in the lamplight. There was no doubt about it; the blood was black. The stains on the metal looked like smears of unrefined oil.

"My God…" Maggie stammered.

"Maybe it's a disease or something," Audrey said. "You should go wash your face, Aunt Maggie. I'll get Mr. Hanson into the bedroom."

Maggie nodded as she continued to look at the knife blade in disbelief. What sort of disease could cause a person's blood to turn black? And more importantly, could that disease be caught by mere contact? Standing, Maggie walked into the bathroom to wash off her face.

February 13th, 2007

Catchville, Wisconsin

10:16 p.m. CST

        While Seth, Anne and Ronnie maneuvered the dresser from the bedroom to block the apartment door, and Audrey helped Skip into bed, Dizzy went into the living room and sat down on one of the folding chairs. Without thinking about it, his arthritic fingers reached into his shirt pocket and pulled out his pack of Camels. For the first time in a long time, Dizzy Vaughn's mind was a blank. Contrary to popular belief, Dizzy's head was usually doing a half-past a hundred. Sometimes it got so bad that he had to pick up one of the tattered Zane Grey paperbacks he kept in the drawer of the nightstand next to his bed, or one of the *National Geographics* he'd subscribed to since August of 1969. When the running in his mind got bad, Dizzy just had to occupy it with something, and usually a good book or magazine would do the trick. Sometimes, though, sometimes the thinkin' wouldn't quit. Sometimes his mind would just keep on runnin' until Dizzy thought his head would explode. It wasn't until he reached into his forties that he sort of realized that all that thinkin'—enough of it so he couldn't sleep sometimes—probably wasn't normal. When he told Less about it, the gas station owner suggested that maybe Dizzy ought to see a doctor. The topic was crossed over with no more seriousness than the discussion of the price of milk, and Dizzy had waved off the advice. Sure, there were some nights when he couldn't sleep and there were other times where he couldn't stop thinking unless he started to read, but it wasn't bad enough to go see a doctor.

        When Dizzy's mind started to run, it really didn't focus on any one thing. One second he'd be thinking about how the hell he was gonna get any wood chopped for his fireplace with his 'thritis rearing up so bad. The next he'd be thinking about how he'd better get over to the station and pick up a carton of smokes before they closed if he didn't want to run out. He'd barely have that thought out of his head before another would swim in and take its place. Dizzy knew that lots of time people thought he was just plain dumb. He knew that they'd see him sittin' on his barstool in the station, or sittin' on his other barstool over at the tavern, and they'd wonder how a man who usually didn't say more than ten words in an hour couldn't be dumb. He wasn't dumb. He wasn't talking because his mind was going a mile a minute, and sometimes it'd get so bad that he just couldn't get a word in edgewise.

Ah, well, it was just a fact of life. It was just who he was.

But now, as he sat down on the folding chair in the living room of Maggie's apartment with a lit cigarette on his lower lip, Dizzy's mind was an absolute blank. He was staring across the room at the blank television set, zoning out. So static was his mind that he didn't realize that he hadn't taken a tug off his smoke for going on two minutes. Dizzy just sat and stared. For the first time in a long time Dizzy Vaughn's mind just didn't want to think about what was going on.

Maggie finished washing her face and went into the bedroom to check on Skip. She found Audrey at the bedside, and Ronnie, Seth and Anne standing inside the door. "Excuse me," she said, moving past them. "How are you, Skip?"

This time when he swallowed, his teeth clenched. "Dresser?"

"It's in front of the door, Skip," Ronnie said. "That 'bino ain't getting through, least not so we don't know he's coming."

Seth cleared his throat in a way that called all their attention to him. He locked eyes with Skip and an unspoken thought ran between them. Skip nodded from the bed and Seth spoke. "We can't stay here."

The eyes of the others went wide and it was, of course, Ronnie who protested first.

"What the fuck do you mean we can't stay here?"

In any other situation Seth might have yelled at the man. Since they'd met him, Ronnie Eaves had been nothing but obnoxious through his endless complaints. But Seth didn't yell at him. Perhaps it was because of what he just saw in the lobby of the Bennington Hotel, or perhaps because of what he felt when he grabbed onto that arm jutting through the hole in the door. It could have been those things, but what it really was, was an essential need for the others to hear and understand him. He had to convince them, and Seth knew he couldn't do it by yelling at Ronnie Eaves.

"We're as good as trapped here," Seth's voice was low but controlled. He felt that it was essential to keep it under control. He had to act as if he was sure of what he spoke, even if the truth was that he wasn't. "We're like a bunch of rabbits trapped in a hole. Whoever's out there, *what*-ever's out there, I don't think it's just going to leave us alone. I think it means to come back and get us one by one."

It was Audrey who spoke up. "But we're safe here. We've got the gun, we've got the door locked and the dresser propped up in front of it... why would we leave? We're safe!"

Seth shook his head before she finished speaking. He looked at his watch. "We've got nine hours—give or take—before the sun comes up. In that time our defenses are going to go down. Whether it's by sleep or boredom or whatever, sooner or later that albino is going to come through that door, and when it does we're gonna be trapped."

"Haven't you heard a damn word she said?" Ronnie's eyes had taken on a wild look. "We're safe here. If that 'bino comes back through the door, we shoot it. Simple as that!"

The urge to yell at this hick-local bubbled to the surface. Instead, Seth closed his eyes and took in deep breath. When he let that breath back out and opened his eyes, Seth felt calmer and surer of himself. "Ronnie," he began, his voice even lower than it had been, "you saw that thing. You felt how cold it was. You saw when the knife cut it how it didn't react. You saw its eyes in the lobby. You saw the black blood on Maggie's face… on the floor. You of all people should realize that we're nowhere near safe."

Ronnie's eyes started to squint again as Seth spoke. If Seth had been yelling, he wouldn't have listened to more than a few words. If Seth had been yelling, Ronnie's defenses would have gone up and he would have started thinking about what kind of insults he could yell back. But Seth hadn't yelled. Seth had spoken slowly and calmly, and without a hint of hostility. To Ronnie, the college professor that had come into Catchville only a few hours earlier with his college professor wife, had made some sense. Ronnie *had* felt the cold. Ronnie *had* seen the arm stay strong during that first knife blow. Ronnie *had* seen the glowing blue eyes and the black blood.

Averting his gaze from Seth's, Ronnie looked down at Skip on the bed. Skip was staring at him with a look that said he knew as much as Ronnie did. Skip nodded and Ronnie nodded back.

"He's right. We're not safe here." Ronnie blew out the breath of a condemned man.

Maggie, who had been listening to this with uncharacteristic silence, finally spoke up. "Now just wait a minute," she looked at Seth, "where do you expect us to go? Right now the lower level of the Bennington's the only place that's got any heat."

"The rooms are out," Ronnie said. "We'd be just as trapped in there as we are in here."

Audrey pointed to the far wall of the bedroom. "How about the dining room. There's two ways out of there?"

Seth shook his head. "Too many windows. If that thing can plunge its hands through a solid oak door, it'll have no problem getting in through a window."

"But we'll hear it coming," Maggie protested. "It anything comes through a window we'll just shoot it… that is," a darkness came over Maggie's eyes, a certain, knowing darkness. "That is unless you think shooting it won't do any good, Mr. Landon?"

The two of them looked at each other with growing dread.

"That is what you think, isn't it?"

Seth tore his eyes away from her. "I don't want to jump to conclusions. But let's consider what we know. The arm I felt, the same arm that Ronnie felt, was colder than ice. The eyes of it were, I don't know exactly how to explain it, they were…"

"Like deer eyes," Ronnie said. "Like deer eyes in the headlights of your car."

Seth nodded. "The eyes didn't look right. Let's leave it at that. We know that its blood is black… all I'm saying is that we don't really know what we're up against. He could be sick. He could have some sort of disease,"

"Like rabies?" Audrey asked.

"I guess so."

"All right," Maggie said. "You've made your point, but where are we going to—"

The eruption of breaking glass from the living room sounded like an explosion in the apartment. Audrey and Anne screamed. Skip turned his head towards the door and then winced in pain. Ronnie, Seth and Maggie all stared at one another—each waiting for the other to make the first move.

Breaking through all of this was a soft moan coming from the living room. Maggie was the first to realize what it was. "Dizzy!" She started towards the door.

"Wait!" Seth said, "Where's the gun?"

Maggie thought for less than a second. "On the table in the kitchen."

Seth turned and glanced into the hall. From the direction

of the living room, the sounds of breaking glass had diminished to a rough tinkling. Dizzy Vaughn still moaned, but now it sounded like a veiled scream. Seth stepped up the hall and grabbed the gun from the table. If he would have thought for a moment, he might have realized that it wasn't loaded, but he didn't think. All he was worried about right now was finding out what was happening in the living room without getting killed.

"Careful, Seth," Anne said from the bedroom as he passed. She was wearing her fear on her face like pain. He gave her a cursory nod before moving down the remainder of the hall. Dizzy's cries were now reduced to strangled yelps. Here at the edge of the living room, Seth could smell the sharp stink of Dizzy's cigarette and feel the dull cold sneaking in through the broken window.

Seth took a second to inhale. He gripped the rifle, brought its butt up to his shoulder and stepped around the corner just in time to see the bottoms of Dizzy Vaughn's shoes slip out through the window into the dark.

The window—with ragged shards of glass still hanging at its edges—looked like a hellish hole leading into outer space. As soon as Dizzy's shoes were gone, a blast of snow rode the cold wind into the living room. Seth only stared at the window for the moment, and as such he didn't realize right away that the room was on fire.

February 9th, 2007

Chequamegon National Forest, Wisconsin

1:21 p.m. CST

The frozen rabbit lay at the base of a birch tree, its head cracked in two like a walnut. Helman Graff knew it had taken his prey less than two seconds to dispense of the animal once he'd caught it. The rabbit was nothing more than an appetizer, a snack of sorts. The skull had been snapped open with the canines, the contents slurped out, and the animal carcass discarded like a candy wrapper.

Timothy was running out of food, and that was a very, very bad thing. He was running his way across the country on instinct, and by that same instinct he would avoid human contact at all cost.

At almost all cost.

Timothy's hunger was something that couldn't be avoided. He'd gorge himself on cattle, horses, deer, rabbit, and even bear for as long as he could, but sooner or later he would need to taste man once more. Helman had hoped that that occasion would come later—much later—but the lack of easy prey in the forest was going to force Timothy into a populated area.

And then what?

And then all hell would break loose.

Helman started up the Polaris Black Widow and gunned the throttle. There were no tracks near the rabbit's frozen corpse. Timothy had a few days on him, Helman was sure of that. The problem was that with the lack of easy prey in the forest, Timothy might not hold to his east-southeasterly course. In his hunger, he might head north, south, east… hell, he might even start to backtrack west.

The sound of the snowmobile ricocheted off of the trees like barbed wire. Helman told himself he'd continue to look for any sign of Timothy through nightfall. If he couldn't find any, he'd have to head to the nearest town to question the locals and read the obituaries.

February 13th, 2007

Catchville, Wisconsin

10:33 p.m. CST

The freezing wind coming in through the broken windows fanned the flames licking up the drapes. When Dizzy had been unceremoniously pulled outside, one of his feet kicked over the kerosene lamp that had been sitting on the end table.

"Fire!" Seth yelled. "Fire!"

Anne and Ronnie came up to Seth's side. The three of them stared at the broken window with wide eyes. While they watched, the flames from the drapes caught on the antique sofa. With an audible *whoosh*, the piece of furniture was ablaze. Seth, Anne and Ronnie put their arms in front of their faces and backed out of the living room.

"Watch out!" Maggie yelled as she moved past them, holding a small red fire extinguisher she'd gotten from the kitchen. Maggie stepped fully into the living room, which was filling fast with bulbous gray plumes of smoke. The Bennington's structure was mostly wood, and that wood was ripe to burn. Even as Maggie unleashed the white foam spray from the extinguisher, the flames were already catching along the wall and ceiling.

"Ronnie! Seth!" Maggie called, still spraying the flames. "There's a bigger fire extinguisher out in the lobby! Go get it!"

The two men looked at each other for a moment. The same thought was running through their heads: What if the crazy guy was out there?

Maggie saw their hesitation over her shoulder. "What are you two waiting for? Take the gun and get the extinguisher!"

Seth moved first. Holding the gun at his side he raced past

Anne and now Audrey down the hall. "Help me move this!" he cried, grabbing onto the edge of the dresser with one hand.

Audrey, Ronnie and Seth all crowded around the dresser and pulled it away from the door. Over the roar of the flames from the other room they could hear the dresser's legs scraping across the hardwood floor.

"Ready?" Seth asked Ronnie. The other man nodded.

"Here," Audrey said, handing Ronnie a flashlight. He shined it through the hole in the door.

"Well?" Seth asked.

"I don't see anything…" Ronnie's voice sounded unsure.

"Let's go." Seth opened up the door and held the gun in front of his chest. He felt, more than saw Anne start to follow him. "No," he said, turning to her. "Stay here, hon."

"But…"

"No buts. Stay here. You too, Audrey. Close the door behind us."

All of them heard Maggie yell from the living room. "Audrey! Tell them to hurry up!"

Seth moved into the anteroom behind the lobby's desk and motioned for Ronnie to follow. When both of them had stepped fully into the anteroom they heard the apartment door shut behind them.

Looking around the corner of the doorway into the lobby, Seth could feel his heart pumping at his temples. He had a moment to realize that he was terrified as Ronnie shined the flashlight towards the front doors of the Bennington. All was quiet. Ronnie switched hands and shined the light at the French doors that led into the dining room. Again, all was clear. Seth moved around the front desk and almost tripped on the smashed cash register. He stepped over it and started to scan the walls for the extinguisher.

"Where is it?"

Ronnie shined the light at waist level on all the walls. "Shit, I've buh-buh-been in here about a tri-tri-trillion times and I don't remember ever seein' one." The man's voice was shaky with panic.

"Seth!" Anne's voice came from behind them. Both of the men jumped in the lobby.

Anne continued. "Maggie says hurry! The fire's getting out of control!"

Seth stepped to his right so that he could see down the wide hallway that led to the rooms. "Shine the light down there."

Ronnie did and both of them saw a fire extinguisher attached to the wall about halfway down.

"Go get it," Ronnie said. When Seth looked at him, Ronnie averted his eyes. "I'll stay here and shine the light down the hall.

Of course you will you spineless dog, Seth thought before replying, "Fine."

Holding the gun in front of his chest, Seth sprinted down the hall towards the extinguisher. He was breathing hard by the time he reached it. Seth sat the gun down for only a moment as he unhooked the heavy, red apparatus from the wall. Grunting, Seth tucked it under one arm and picked up the gun with the other.

When he turned back towards the lobby, Seth was momentarily blinded as Ronnie pointed the flashlight directly at him.

"Hey!" Seth yelled, squinting. "Point that thing somewhere else!"

Ronnie pointed the light at the ground as a momentous crash of glass sounded from the lobby. Seth stopped, blinking his eyes, and watched as Ronnie spun in the direction of the Bennington's dining room.

Screaming, Ronnie put his hands up, palms out. Seth watched as something dove into his field of vision and tackled Ronnie around the midsection. He only caught a quick glimpse of the attacker, but Seth was certain that he saw the white hair before Ronnie was pushed towards the lobby doors and out of Seth's sight.

Seth hesitated. He looked down at the gun in his right hand and still he hesitated. Here it was: the final confrontation. Sighing, he put the extinguisher down on the hallway floor and gripped the shotgun with two, shaking hands.

From the lobby, Ronnie continued to scream.

Seth jogged to the end of the hallway and stopped. He could see the flashlight lying on the floor where Ronnie had stood only seconds ago. From his left, out of his line of sight, Ronnie's screams began to diminish. They were replaced by an oddly wet, guttural sound that Seth tried to block from his mind. From the anteroom behind the lobby's desk, Seth heard Audrey and Anne screaming. *Just stay there*, he wanted to cry out. *Just stay there and be quiet.* But he didn't dare shout to them. The thing that was attacking Ronnie might not know that Seth was there, and he wanted to keep it that way.

Gripping his eyes tightly shut and holding the length of the gun's barrel up near his face, the image of Less Huggard's broken body lying in the red light of the Amoco gas station hallway came to Seth's mind. He opened his eyes to rid himself of the image, took a deep breath, and stepped around the corner.

February 13th, 2007

Catchville, Wisconsin

10:38 p.m. CST

The memory of the top of Less Huggard's head severed above the ears was nothing compared to what Seth now saw.

Ronnie was dead. There was no doubt about it. He sat upright only because the man—*the thing*—was holding him so. The thing with the white hair, pale skin, and foggy blue eyes knelt at Ronnie's side, biting into the man's forehead as if it were a ripe melon.

Seth watched as Ronnie's blood rolled down in enormous drips over his eyes, nose and chin. The thing that bit into Ronnie was covered in blood as well, but only from the mouth down. The blood on its neck and hands presumably wasn't only Ronnie's, some of that red stuff was probably Dizzy's as well.

The thing tore its mouth away from Ronnie's head and a large chunk of skin and flesh came with it. While the thing chomped that down, it squeezed Ronnie's head at the ears and presently Seth heard a dull *crack* that made him cringe. The next bite came directly at the top of the head. The thing opened its mouth wide, leading with its teeth, and tore away a chocolate chip cookie-sized chunk of hair, skin, and skull.

Seth's stomach lurched as the thing dug its fingers into the edges of the hole it had made in Ronnie's skull, and *pulled*. The top of Ronnie's head flowered open, producing a whole new cornucopia of blood and brain matter. Seth heard the thing give a low, throaty purr as it reached into that cornucopia and scooped a handful into its mouth.

It was a direct result of witnessing this revolting act more than a mental sense that he had to do something that prompted

Seth to step into the lobby.

The thing stopped in mid-chew and looked up at him with those cloudy, dead eyes.

Seth felt blood pounding in his ears as he brought the shotgun up to his shoulder. The thing snarled and stood, holding its hands at its sides. With the thing no longer supporting it, Ronnie's body fell back to the floor with a thud. There was no doubt about it; the thing was going to attack.

Aiming at the thing's chest, Seth pulled the shotgun's trigger.

Click.

Seth pulled the trigger again as the thing started towards him.

Click.

The gun was empty. Seth's eyes widened out as he alternated his gaze between the gun and the closing man-thing. The thing snarled again and reached out with two bloody hands. Seth fell backwards onto the floor of the lobby, his head connecting with the hardwood hard enough to make him see stars. The thing was close enough now that Seth could smell the foul scent of death on its breath.

Gritting his teeth, Seth felt a blast of cold air. A half a second later he heard a gunshot.

There was no look of surprise on the thing's face as a bullet exploded out the front of its forehead. Seth was stunned, but his horror overrode his shock as the man-thing started falling towards him. Seth rolled out of the way as the thing collapsed to the floor.

The bearded man dressed in black winter clothing knelt down next to Ronnie's body. Vaguely, Seth could hear Anne and Audrey screaming from Maggie's apartment. He realized that he was out of their line of sight and that they had no idea what had just happened.

Seth watched as the bearded man holding the rifle walked over to the dead man-thing on the floor.

"Thank... thanks," Seth stammered.

The man glanced at Seth and then looked down the hall that led to the hotel rooms. "You better get that extinguisher and put the fire out."

February 13th, 2007

Catchville, Wisconsin

10:51 p.m. CST

There was a lot of smoke, but Maggie and Seth managed to put out the fire using the two extinguishers. When they walked back out into the lobby accompanied by Anne and Skip, Audrey was tentatively standing near the beast that had held Catchville in terror all evening.

"Where is he?" Seth asked.

Audrey turned quickly, as if she felt guilty for looking at the man-thing. "He... he asked me if I knew who else had been killed. I told him about Mrs. Meadows, Mr. Huggard and Dizzy. He took a picture of Ronnie and then..." she pointed to the man with white hair on the floor.

"Why'd he take pictures of them?" Anne asked. Audrey shrugged.

Seth walked over and stood by Maggie's niece. He looked down at the thing that had looked at him with those foggy blue eyes. What had been wrong with him? What disease, whether mental or physical, had he been afflicted with to make him feast on his fellow man?

"Thank God he's dead," Maggie whispered. She stepped forward with Anne and Skip and the five of them stood in a circle around the man-thing, staring.

When the front door to the Bennington flew open they all jumped. An evening of being on edge was taking its toll on all of their nerves. The bearded man dressed in a black winter coat, snow-pants, boots and hat stood looking at them with a rifle slung over his shoulder. Seth had time to think to himself that that thermos-sized scope on top of the rifle had to be some sort of laser or thermal sight.

As the man closed the hotel door, Maggie spoke. "Who are you?"

The man acted as if he hadn't heard her. He stepped around Ronnie's body and pulled off his hat and gloves. "I assume the phones don't work."

"That's right," Maggie said, and then repeated, "Who are you?"

"Is the fire out?" They all nodded that it was and watched as the man unzipped his jacket. He reached inside and pulled out a small, silver flask, unscrewed the cap, and took a short drink.

Hugging herself with her arms, Maggie stepped towards the man. "Tell us who you are."

The stranger took another pull from the flask before screwing the cap back on and replacing it in his jacket. "Who I am doesn't matter." He started pulling his gloves back on his hands. "You folks have some work to do. I found the old man, the one she called Dizzy, behind the hotel. I'd get these two bodies out into the cold for the night. In the case of your friend here," he pointed to Ronnie, "I know it might seem disrespectful, but he's going to start stinking up the joint if you leave him on the floor. Is there any other building with heat?"

Maggie started to shake her head when Skip grunted. They all looked at him while he swallowed hard and whispered, "Dizz... Dizzy's house... fireplace."

"That's right," Maggie said. "Dizzy's house has a working fireplace."

The stranger nodded. "All right," he pointed back towards Maggie's apartment. "If you can't get that window boarded up maybe you can spend the night at the old guy's house, though if you close the door to the apartment, I think the hotel rooms should stay warm enough until morning."

"You're not staying here?" Anne asked.

The stranger shook his head. "Call the police as soon as the phones are up. Tell them exactly what happened."

Seth laughed. "And what did happen?"

Audrey nodded her head and pointed to the dead man with the white hair. "Who was that… maniac?"

Taking a deep breath, the stranger pulled on his hat and looked at the dead man-thing on the floor. "That man is not a maniac. That man's name is Timothy Kail. Remember that name. Timothy Kail. Tell the police he was from Cavalier, North Dakota. He'll be blamed for all these deaths, but he's just as much a victim as the rest of the dead."

The stranger turned and headed for the door. It was Anne who spoke after him.

"What do you mean by that? Where are you going? Who are you?"

He stopped and looked back at them. "I told you, it doesn't matter who I am. As for where I'm going… I'm going to get the person who set this all in motion."

They all looked at the stranger, confused.

"Good night." The man turned and left the Bennington Hotel.

March 31st, 2007

New York, New York

12:04 p.m. EST

Dressed in a suit and tie, Helman Graff walked down a street lined with well-to-do apartments. To the best of his knowledge, the address printed on the piece of paper in his hand was reliable. Businessmen and women brushed by him on the sidewalk, giving him no more notice than anyone else. By appearances, Helman was one of them, a businessman on his way to lunch.

Helman stopped in front of the three-story apartment building, and looked at the address again. The apartment he was looking for was on the second floor. Helman brought up his gaze and through sheer luck locked eyes with a black woman looking out of a second-story window. The woman looked at him for two seconds, three, before backing out of sight.

It was her. Helman was sure of it.

He jogged up the four steps to the building's front door, stuffing the address into his pocket as he went. When his hand came back out of the pocket it held a small knife. This knife couldn't be bought in any sporting goods or department store. The knife Helman held was handmade by a craftsman in Portugal. Helman examined the door lock for a moment before selecting one of the knife's blades and inserting it into the lock. Nineteen grooves along the side of the knife were manipulated quickly, one by one, until the knife turned, turning the lock with it. Helman Graff was inside the building in seconds.

Once inside, he listened, expecting to hear footsteps on either the steps or in the back hall of the lower level, but he heard nothing. Other than a radio playing classical music in one of the first floor apartments, all was quiet.

Satisfied that no one was about, Helman laid his briefcase across the stairwell banister and popped it open. He removed a nine-millimeter pistol equipped with a silencer and closed the case.

The old steps creaked as he climbed them, so Helman didn't hurry. There was an off chance that the woman didn't know who he was and he didn't want to alarm her just yet by running. The top of the stairs ended in a hallway that divided the building. To Helman's right was an apartment door that read 2B. He turned to the left, to the one that read 2A.

There was no reason to knock. If the woman didn't know who he was or why he was here, he'd catch her by surprise. If she did know why she was here, God knew she wouldn't answer when he knocked, and breaking it down instead of picking it might give her a scare as well.

WHAM! Helman threw his shoulder into the door with a solid effort. *WHAM!* He didn't hesitate to give the door a second hit—*WHAM!*—or a third—*WHAM!*—or fourth. The door lock gave on the last hit but was still held by a chain. Helman backed a few feet away from the door, lifted his right leg and kicked the door open wide.

Helman held the gun in front of him with his right hand and the briefcase at his side with his left. Through the door was a small foyer that led to a kitchen.

Listening, Helman judged that no one was in the kitchen. He entered and closed the door behind him. To the right was a walk-in pantry that also served as a laundry room. A small washer was stacked on top of a dryer. Neither was running. Helman looked over at the sink and out the window above it. This was where the woman had been standing when he'd seen her from the street.

From somewhere deeper in the apartment, Helman heard the *click* of a door closing quietly. He wasted no time. In a second he was across the kitchen and into a large living room. Oddly colored rugs and tapestries were spread on the floor and over the furniture. Stringy green plants hung from the ceiling in suspended planters. Several masks made of dried mud and papier-mâché adorned the walls. Beaded drapes covered the windows casting green and yellow light across the room. The scent of pungent incense crawled through the air.

Three doors led out of the living room but only one of them was closed. Helman headed straight for it. Setting his briefcase down on the floor, he held the barrel of the nine-millimeter up to his ear and grasped the knob with his free hand. He turned the knob, threw open the door and pointed his gun dead ahead all in one fluid motion. There she was; the woman who had dominated Helman's thoughts for the last five months leaned against the dresser on the far side of the bedroom. She looked different from the pictures Helman had collected in his research. Whereas in the pictures her hair was a curly brown bob, now it was tied into shoulder-length black braids. Even from where he stood, Helman could tell that the woman had changed her eye color from brown to green with some sort of colored contact lenses. Fear showed in the expression of those eyes… fear and something else.

"Hello Margarite," Helman said, glancing to the left and right to be sure there was no one else in the bedroom. There wasn't.

The woman's Haitian Creole accent was thick. "How did you find me?"

"I have my sources—"

Before Helman finished his sentence, one of the woman's hands shot out from behind her back and flung a knife through the air. If Helman hadn't moved as quickly as he did, the knife would have pegged him in the center of the chest. As it happened, the knife caught him in the right shoulder.

As he fell to the side, Helman was aware of the woman making a run for it. Mentally willing away the pain, he stood, reached up with his left hand and grabbed a handful of the woman's braids. Her head jerked backwards as Helman threw her head to the floor as if he were spiking a football. For Margarite, all went black.

March 31st, 2007

New York, New York

12:29 p.m. EST

Margarite awoke with a severe throbbing filtering down from the top of her head. She rolled onto her side and from the lack of give beneath her body she assumed she was on the floor. Opening her eyes, she saw that indeed she was on the floor of her living room. The multi-colored rug she'd purchased in her beloved Port au-Prince stretched away from her eyes to the far wall.

"Get up." The man's voice seemed to reach her ears through a mile of water. Margarite rolled onto her stomach and brought her knees underneath her with extreme effort. She turned her head and saw the bearded man wearing the suit sitting on the couch, his right shoulder wrapped with a torn section of sheet from her bed. In front of him on the coffee table sat his opened briefcase. Positioned the way it was, its contents were hidden from her. Though her head was still pounding, Margarite stood. She could now see that the man's right hand still held the pistol.

"Who are you?"

He shook his head. "I get to ask the questions." Leaning forward, the man pulled a manila folder from the briefcase and opened it up. "You are Margarite Kail. Formerly Margarite Dejeun. Correct?"

Margarite remained silent as the man continued to look at the folder.

"Your grandmother, Monique, was a Voodoo Priestess, specifically referred to as a *mambo*. Is that correct?"

Silence.

"When your parents were killed in 1995, your grandmother

took you in and taught you the tools of the trade. Correct?"

Silence.

"You came to the United States in 2000 to live with your cousin in North Dakota. In January of 2002 you met Timothy Kail. In August of 2002 you married him." He paused. "I wonder if that was out of true love or a need for citizenship."

Margarite opened her mouth to speak but the man held up his gun, stopping her.

"Don't answer. It has no bearing on what we're doing here."

She put her hands on her hips. "And what exactly is it that we're doing here?"

The man looked up at her with sparkling brown eyes. His expression was emotionless. "Judgement."

The fear that Margarite felt when she first spotted the man on the sidewalk returned ten-fold as he continued to speak.

"Between December of 2002 and September of 2006 you were admitted to the Pembina County hospital emergency room twenty-six times with broken fingers and toes, a smashed-in nose, a dislocated shoulder, lacerations on your back and breasts, numerous black eyes and split lips, and a sprained ankle. In October of 2006 you broke into the Fins & Things fish store in Cavalier, North Dakota and stole a Fugu Puffer fish."

The man stopped looking at the file and fixed his gaze on her. "I wonder what Timothy thought what you brought home that fish. You didn't kill him until nine days later so you had to have kept the fish alive at least until then…"

Margarite said nothing. Her thoughts were racing to find a way out of this. Whoever this man was, he wasn't with the police. The police could never have put Margarite's particular puzzle together with any degree of success. Whoever this man was, he was dangerous.

The man shrugged at her lack of an answer. "No matter. After killing Timothy in that car crash, I'm guessing that you performed your zombification ritual when you visited him in the Pembina County morgue as the grieving widow. 'May I please have a few minutes alone with my husband', is that how it went? Don't answer. No one stole Timothy's body. Timothy got up and walked out on his own. Shortly after your visit to the morgue, you fled east, knowing full well that Timothy would have no choice but to follow. Correct?" The man waited for an answer this time, staring at her with those damned brown eyes.

Margarite took a deep breath. "You've no idea what that man did to me."

"Considering the amount of times you visited the emergency room, I think I do. What I don't understand is why you weren't satisfied with just killing him. What I don't understand is why you made him wander across the country thinking of only food in the form of living brain tissue, survival, and finding you."

Shaking her head through all of this, Margarite finally brought up her hands to cover her eyes. She thought back to all the times she'd been pinned in the corner of the apartment in Cavalier. She thought back to all the times she's been punched and kicked until she retched on the carpet. She thought back to all the times Tim dragged a knife across her back and stomach, laughing all the while.

Margarite thought back to the nightmare of a life she'd lived with that animal.

She brought her hands down and her eyes glared with a new intensity. "You have no idea," she repeated, shaking her head.

The man raised his chin. "Oh, but I do." Again he reached into his briefcase. This time he pulled out a stack of 4X6 photos.

"What are those?" The trepidation in Margarite's voice was apparent.

"They're yours." He held them out to her.

Slowly, Margarite reached out and took the pictures. She thumbed through only two before holding them at her side. The bodies in the first two pictures—one of an orange-clad hunter bloody from the neck up, and a naked, mutilated body on a gurney that was far too well lit—threatened to turn Margarite's stomach.

"Look at them, Margarite." The slightest bit of anger began to seep into the man's voice. "Look at your victims. Look at the sixteen people dead by your hand. Look at the animals, including livestock and family pets that died by your hand. Look at the death you spread across three different states."

Margarite began to shake her head back and forth. This was a distraction, a feint. Her grandmother had always taught her to lead with her weak hand, to start with the weakest concoction, and that practice was ingrained. She scrunched up her face and made to cry. As the man's mouth opened to say something else, Margarite threw the stack of pictures at him like a Frisbee.

The pictures split in the air, separating like confetti above the coffee table. Margarite never saw this. As soon as the pictures left her hand she turned and sprinted towards the kitchen. She actually thought she was going to make it, she thought she was going to get to the front door and escape when a strange, twisting sound reached her ears a fraction of a second before her right leg felt like it was punched from behind.

Margarite went down hard on the linoleum of the kitchen floor, her cheek squeaking against it as she slid. The man grabbed one of her shoulders and flipped Margarite onto her back. He crouched down and pinned her with his knees. The tip of the gun's silencer was placed against her temple.

"How did you find me? Who are you?" Margarite spat.

The man took a deep breath. "You might call this a hobby of mine. I watch the internet and the newspapers for signs of crimes that may not be detected by regular law enforcement. I look for things like animal sacrifice. I look for things like odd church vandalism. I look for things like transient murders that all take place during a full moon. I look for things like crop circles. I look for things that are used in zombification rituals... like Fugu Puffer fish.

"My name is Helman Graff. If you would've just killed Timothy and left it at that, you would never have known I exist. God knows the scumbag probably deserved it. I do have compassion for what you endured from him. However, you didn't leave it at that. Using the ancient rituals taught to you by your grandmother, you turned him into a zombie. Didn't you?"

The anger, fear, and frustration were coming to a boil behind Margarite's eyes. She had a moment to realize that the pain in her leg was throbbing dully, she had another moment to realize that when she saw this man from her kitchen window, she should have run out the back door.

"Didn't you?" the man yelled, pushing the tip of the silencer harder into her temple.

"Yes!" Margarite's eyes narrowed. "And I'd do it again!"

The man nodded. "I know you would. Margarite Kail, for the zombification of your husband, and for the ensuing deaths of at least sixteen people, for the trauma and fear and nightmares to come that you inflicted on countless others, Margarite Kail, I sentence you to death.

Margarite opened her mouth to scream, but the time for screaming had passed.

Helman Graff pulled the trigger.

November 29th, 2008

Eau Claire, Wisconsin

1:08 p.m. CST

Maggie Bennington gripped the wheel harder as she turned her car into the Sacred Heart Hospital parking lot. The call she received this morning had made her close down the bar and head straight for Eau Claire. The roads had been clear and Maggie drove faster than she ever had in her entire life. She found a parking spot and jogged into the hospital lobby.

"Anne Landon's room!" Maggie said, out of breath, to the receptionist.

Maggie tapped her fingers on the counter while the young woman looked at the computer and gave her the room number.

When the elevator doors opened, Maggie saw Seth walking down the hall. She went to him, and as she got closer he could see the puffy redness under his eyes. He'd been crying.

"Seth!"

He looked up at her and gave her a hug. "I'm so glad you came."

"How is she?" Maggie asked, still feeling out of breath. "How is Anne?"

Without saying a word, he turned and led her down the hall. Maggie held her breath as he opened the door and stood aside. What she saw when she entered was enough to cause Maggie to tear up as well.

Anne lay in the hospital bed holding onto a swaddled baby.

"Oh, Anne!" Maggie exclaimed, the tears coming in force

now. "What is it?"

Anne smiled. "It's a girl."

Walking over to the bedside, Maggie held her arms out. Anne handed the tiny bundle over to the woman. Maggie looked down at the child who was oblivious to the events that happened on the night she was conceived.

"She's beautiful," Maggie whispered. "Just beautiful. What's her name?"

Seth and Anne exchanged a glance. Seth nodded to Anne who said, "We've named her Margaret, or Maggie for short."

Acknowledgements

I would like to thank a number of people for their help and support in making this book possible.

First, thanks to my Pre-Readers, a number of hand-selected friends who have suffered through my many manuscripts. Thanks to Jed Schilling, Brent Knutson, Paul Nemec, Brian Ristola, Marcia Borgen, Lori Pacovsky and Ren Richfield.

Second, let me offer a huge thanks to Lisa Lenmark, who especially helped me out with the development of this particular book, and to Kristofer J. Stamp, my esteemed benefactor.

Of course, the greatest amount of thanks goes to Lisa, Lauren and Hayden; they are the triumvirate that keeps me on the straight and narrow.

Scott F. Falkner

February 23rd, 2006

Visit StoneGarden.Net Publishing Online!

You can find us at: www.stonegarden.net, the book shop is available from: http://bookshop.stonegarden.net.

News and Upcoming Titles

New titles and reader favorites are featured each month, along with information on our upcoming titles.

Author Info

Author bios, blogs and links to their personal websites.

Contests and Other Fun Stuff

Web forum to keep in touch with your favorite authors, autographed copies and more!

Dark Horror from

Robert Starr

◘ Creek Water   (0-9765426-9-2 -$6.99 US)

Rob's stories have a way of catching you that you least expect. At
first, you think the hero is a madman, searching for spirits of "joy"
in the woods. Then you realize he was describing a feeling of
connection with the world around him just as you might get if you
were to watch a bald eagle take flight from just above your head as
you canoe across a lake. It's that feeling of oneness with the
universe, that hopeful notion that the world is some wondrous
process that will turn out right in spite of anything we mere
humans do to muck it up. (Nathan Kailhofer-Author)

StoneGarden.Net Publishing

3851 Cottonwood Dr., Danville, CA   94506

Please send me the **StoneGarden.net Publishing** book I have checked above. I
am enclosing $_____ (check, money order for US residents only, VISA and
Mastercard accepted—no currency or COD's). Please include the list price plus
$3 per order to cover handling costs ($5 outside of the US). Prices and numbers
are subject to change without notice. (Prices slightly higher in Canada.)

Name:_____

Address:_____

City:_____State:_____Zip:_____Country:_____

VISA/Mastercard:_____

Exp. Date and CVS Code:_____ /_____

Please allow 4-6 weeks for delivery.

Printed in the United States
150829LV00001B/19/A